FIC
BRO

AUTHOR BROWN, JACKIE

TITLE LITTLE CRICKET

2004

DATE DUE	BORROWER'S NAME	ROOM NUMBER
	Kate	4
	Hannah	4

DEMCO

LITTLE cricket

JACKIE BROWN

Hyperion Books for Children
New York

ACKNOWLEDGMENTS

Special thanks to Donna Bray
for her patience and encouragement,
and also to Dr. Chou Chang,
who generously shared his time and knowledge
of the Hmong culture.

Copyright © 2004 by Jackie Brown

Printed in the United States of America
First Edition
1 3 5 7 9 10 8 6 4 2

The text for this book is set in 14-point Mrs. Eaves.
Reinforced binding

Library of Congress Cataloging-in-Publication data on file.
ISBN 0-7868-1852-2

Visit www.hyperionbooksforchildren.com

For Robert,
the wind beneath my wings

Tsuv txaij tes txaij dlaim tawv,
Tuabneeg txaij tes txaij lub plawv.

The stripe of a tiger is apparent to the eye,
But the character of a person
   is hidden deep inside.

                        —Hmong proverb

PROLOGUE

Twelve-year-old Kia Vang stooped down and studied the tiny seeds nestled in the narrow dirt furrow. If she squeezed her eyes tightly shut until little sunbursts of yellow danced behind her lids, she could imagine herself back in her mountain village in Laos. Gone was the apartment building she lived in now with Grandfather and her fourteen-year-old brother, Xigi, and its ugly, dirty windows that looked like unblinking eyes watching her every move. If she tried hard enough, even the never-ending drone of car tires on the busy street in front of their building disappeared.

In her mind Kia heard the soft snuffle of pigs and the self-important cluck of chickens pecking in the dirt around the bamboo hut. And, best of all, she was no longer alone. The sparkling laughter of her cousins rang in the clear mountain air as they helped the women drop rice seeds in the holes. She smiled when she remembered the speckled chicken that insisted upon sitting on her mother's shoulder as she worked, its round, feathered body swaying with each swing of her mother's strong, brown arms.

As unwelcome as a pinch on the arm, the shrill bleat of a car horn startled Kia, and her eyes snapped open. Across the street two girls were scratching the concrete sidewalk with a sharp stone, then hopping on one foot. They lived in the building next to Kia. Whenever Kia passed them they would giggle and whisper words Kia did not understand.

Sometimes, when she was watching them from her upstairs living-room window, she would see the sun glint off their shining hair as they jumped, and she would smile and pretend they were waiting for her to come and play with them. But after a few minutes the smile would slip away because she knew they were not really waiting for her. She knew it was just make-believe.

I

Kia spread her sticky arms and legs out on her sleeping mat to catch the slight breeze that puffed through the open doorway of the hut. Already a thin film of sweat covered them. She listened to the chatter of the morning birds and wondered why the jungle humidity never made them tired as it did people. They always found something to gossip about. Maybe, she thought, shoving her black hair off her forehead with the back of her hand, it was cooler to be covered in feathers and flit among the branches of the trees than to be cooped up in huts where the heat sat on your chest like a ripe melon.

Without opening her eyes, she knew her mother was making egg rolls and spicy meat today. The tangy smell made the back of her mouth water and her nose tingle. It was a treat to have them anytime other than the Hmong New Year because usually Kia's mother was far too busy to make these delicacies. But the weather had been fine, and planting had gone well this year. The harvest was in and the weeds had not yet had time to flourish, so many women of the village had more time to cook and make items to sell at the village market.

Kia rolled off her mat, washed her face and hands in a bucket of water, and sat by her mother as she finished mixing the ingredients for the meat. Grandmother sat just outside the hut, nimble fingers weaving the tough grasses Kia helped her gather to make baskets.

Since she was a girl, Kia's grandmother had made baskets woven from grasses and bamboo to sell at the market. These strong baskets could be used for many years to carry corn and vegetables at harvest time. Even people from other villages came to buy them because they were made so well. Grandmother said she was able to make such good baskets because each time she cut down grasses or bamboo she asked the spirits to guide her hands as she made them. She told Kia that if one were thankful and humble, the spirits would be kind and helpful, but if the spirits were forgotten or ignored, they would think the person who cut them proud and vain.

Kia's mother handed Kia one of Grandmother's sturdy baskets. "When you go with Grandfather this morning, get me some *tauj* so I can make more brooms before the next market day."

After a hasty breakfast of rice noodles and dried fish, Kia went to find her grandfather. She found him outside gazing up at the wispy trails of clouds that would soon burn off in the jungle heat. Kia loved the early mornings. Her eyes traveled over the distant pink mountaintops and shadowed valleys. Behind her, the cows plodded about the village streets and people wound their way down the path to the sluggish river. Children giggled and chased one another while the speck-led chicken spread itself to rest in the dust behind their hut. The smoke from the morning cooking fires melted into the air.

"You and I need to race the sun up the mountain, Little Cricket. There are many plants I need to gather before the sun bakes them."

In the cool of the morning Kia and her grandfather walked hand in hand as they searched the lush mountaintop for the herbs Grandfather used as medicine. He would cut them into thin slices and dry them in a net that hung from the ceiling of their hut. Nearly every day someone came to him for advice on when to plant crops or where to build a house or how to cure an itchy rash that wouldn't go away. When sickness came, Grandfather would choose the right plant to make the sick person well. Sometimes the person had to chew the leaves; sometimes the herb was cooked with a chicken. She watched him walk slowly ahead of her, care-fully searching under leaves and grasses, then placing the plants in a small basket.

"May I go visit Aunt Zoua for a little

while?" Kia asked. Aunt Zoua lived in a rickety hut that clung to the mountainside like a gnat to the side of a water buffalo. The old hut creaked and groaned a little more with each strong wind. Aunt Zoua was not really Kia's aunt, but the whole village called her this because she was so old and had no family left to care for her. Her only son had died when he was an infant. Many times people had tried to persuade her to move off the mountainside into the village where she would be safer, but Aunt Zoua stubbornly insisted on living in the leaky hut that nearly washed down into the valley each rainy season. Everyone loved the old woman, and there wasn't a child in the village that hadn't been bounced upon her knee or rocked in her thin, ropy arms. The old woman couldn't see well anymore, and Kia often stopped to help her.

"Yes, but only for a short while," replied Grandfather, straightening up and stretching his back. "We have much to do today."

The old woman's face broke into a broad, toothless smile when she saw Kia skipping down the steep dirt path toward the hut. The basket slung across Kia's back slapped happily up and down. Aunt Zoua was trying to pound rice with a pestle to make flour, but Kia could see she was not strong enough anymore to crack the husk from the rice grain. The rice just skittered around and around in the earthen bowl like fleas on a dog.

"Would you like me to do that for you?" Kia asked. Aunt Zoua gratefully handed Kia the bowl and pestle and seemed content to just sit and gaze down the mountain into the valley below, her faded eyes hardly more than slits in her wrinkled, brown face.

After a long silence, Aunt Zoua looked up at Kia and asked, "Is your grandfather on the mountain?"

Kia's arm was getting tired, but she looked with satisfaction at the husked rice. "Yes. He is looking for plant medicine today as always."

Mashing her gums together and nodding, the old woman said, "He knows much about making people well. We are lucky to have such a good shaman in our village." As she spoke, Aunt Zoua pointed to her right ankle where, the year before, a venomous snake had bitten her. A villager had stopped by to visit and had found her unconscious on the floor of the hut, her leg purple and swollen to the size of a tree trunk.

Kia's grandfather had been quickly summoned to perform the Hmong healing ceremony. Grandfather had said Aunt Zoua was sick because one of her souls had been frightened away by the snake poison and had to be coaxed back into the body to make it whole again.

Many villagers had crowded into Aunt Zoua's hut to watch Grandfather perform the *hu plig*. For nearly an hour, Grandfather had talked to the spirits and had gone into a deep trance where he trembled so much that Kia thought the old hut would surely tumble down the mountainside. As he talked to the spirits, Grandfather shook a large, circular rattle to help the soul return to Aunt Zoua's body. He tied strings around Aunt Zoua's wrists to keep her recaptured soul in her body so it would not run away and make her sick again. Then he lit two big, smoky torches that lit up the inside of the hut as if the sun had been brought indoors.

By the next day Aunt Zoua's leg was better and she was hobbling around, telling all who would listen of the great powers of Kia's grandfather.

At last, Kia finished pounding the rice and placed the bowl in Aunt Zoua's lap. Clutching Kia's brown hand, Aunt Zoua lifted her old face up to Kia and whispered, "Tell your grandfather to ask the good spirits to make this war go away so our people do not have to move again."

Kia did not know what war was or how to make it go away, but surely Grandfather would know. She slipped her hand from Aunt Zoua's grasp. "I will tell him what you said," Kia promised the old woman. "Now, I must go."

On the way back up the mountain, Kia stopped to admire a magnificent, glistening web spun among the rough grasses. As she put out a finger to touch the silky thread, a fat-bodied brown spider disappeared behind a leaf. "You've been working on this a long time, haven't you?" Kia said softly to the spider. "If ever you get tired of your home here, I will bring you home." Kia believed that if a spider spun a web inside a hut it meant good luck.

Behind her, near the top of the slope, Kia could hear Grandfather humming softly. A feeling of safety and contentment filled her because she knew that when Grandfather hummed he was happy. She stood up, stepped gingerly over the web, and began climbing to the top of the mountain.

"Grandfather, Aunt Zoua says you must ask the spirits to make this war go away. But Grandfather, I don't understand what is happening. Why do we have to keep moving? Father, Uncle Lue, and Aunt Zoua all talk of war and people who want to take over the world to make other people do as they say. But why do they want to do this?" Overhead a soaring bird, looking for its first meal of the day, cast a giant shadow over the steaming ground just as the sun came out.

Grandfather reached under a massive palm tree and pulled up a small plant, roots and all. Gently he tapped it against his leg until a small shower of black dirt left the delicate roots exposed. A sharp, tangy smell drifted up to Kia as he carefully placed the herb in his basket.

"Little Cricket, you should not be

worrying about such things." He called Kia this because she often stood on one skinny, brown leg and rubbed the other behind it, like a cricket. Seeing that his granddaughter was not satisfied with his answer, he continued, "Wars are always about the strong taking from the weak."

Kia wrinkled her forehead in confusion. "Then it is bad to be strong?"

"Only if strength is misused," replied Grandfather. "To be strong is a wonderful thing, but it should be used to help others, not to hurt them."

Kia still did not understand, but before she could ask another question, her grandfather said, "I must collect several more plants yet before the sun finds them. Perhaps you should make use of that basket on your back to collect the *tauj* your mother needs. Cut no more than you can carry. When you are finished, return here and we will go home together."

Up and up Kia climbed until she was where the grasses grew tall as the roof of a hut. From around her waist she unsheathed a sharp knife and began cutting the tough bushes that her mother used to make brooms to sell at the market. The sun was quickly burning off the fog, and Kia stopped for a moment to look across the rippling valleys that were still shrouded in white mist. Sweat stung her eyes as she gently packed the *tauj* in her basket. With great care, she put the knife back in its case. It was razor sharp and could easily cut through bone.

When Kia and Grandfather walked back home, a beautiful orange-and-black butterfly floated beside them for much of the way, then zoomed off toward Aunt Zoua's hut. Kia knew that when a butterfly appeared, it was the soul of a dead person soaring through the sky.

"Grandfather, do you know who I think that butterfly is? I think it is Aunt Zoua's baby come to see if she is all right, since he cannot be here to take care of her himself. Don't you think that, too, Grandfather?"

The old man looked with tenderness at his granddaughter. "That very well might be, and I think he will be very happy to know his mother has such friends as you."

2

Kia's little cousin, Wa, skipped up to her and grabbed her hand and started twirling around.

"Xigi and I are going to the pool to feed the fish. He even said I could throw them some corn if I don't fall in!"

Early as it was, Wa's tan cheeks were already smudged with the black mud that was layered on her hands, packed under her fingernails, and streaked throughout her hair. Kia drew the child close and hugged her. Of her many cousins, Wa was Kia's favorite. The child never stopped smiling, her small, white teeth like kernels of new corn. Kia's grandmother said the good spirits had left a mark of happiness on Wa in the deep dimples that creased each of her round cheeks like embroidered tucks in the beautiful red blouse Grandmother had made her to wear at the New Year's celebration. No one else in Kia's large family could boast of such dimples or eyes the color of wild gingerroot. Kia's eyes were black as the fertile earth of her village.

Wa struggled out of Kia's arms and squatted down beside Xigi, who was sitting cross-legged on the ground next to the hut, drawing.

"Now, Xigi? Can we go now? I've been waiting since tomorrow."

Xigi smiled and stuck his pencil behind his right ear. "Yesterday, Wa. You mean you've been waiting since yesterday," he gently corrected her. When Wa was younger, she thought the pencil grew out of Xigi's ear, but her mother had explained that was where Xigi kept it so it was always handy when he saw something he wanted to draw.

Beaming and nodding, the little girl agreed. "Yes, since yesterday. So can we go now?"

Xigi held up the drawing he had been working on. It was a magnificent tiger padding around a clearing in the forest, ears alert to an unseen sound in the brush. Xigi had drawn the beast so skillfully Kia could almost see the shoulders of the tiger slink up and down as it stalked its prey.

"Do you see this tiger, Wa? It would love to have a little nuisance girl like you to play with, wouldn't it, Kia? If you're not careful, I will take you to the edge of the village where it lies in wait for children like you."

The child's eyes widened and her dimples disappeared. Kia was afraid Xigi had frightened her. Last harvest time, a man who stole a neighbor's pig was thrown out of the village in shame to make his own way in the wild jungle. The children had talked for weeks about whether the man lived or whether a tiger had devoured him. Grandfather had said being cast out from your home and away from fellow human beings was one of the saddest things that could happen to anyone because it meant you were only fit to live with animals.

Wa glanced fearfully at Kia, who pulled her mouth down at the corners and shook her head as if telling her, *I would never let such a thing happen to you.* That was all the encouragement the little girl needed. She whirled back to face Xigi. "Maybe you had better be careful, Xigi, or my papa will throw you out into the jungle for scaring me!" She held up her dirty hands to Xigi, curved them into claws, and gave a mighty roar that silenced the monkeys screeching overhead.

"Oh, yeah?" retorted Xigi, scooping Wa up in his arms, tossing her over his shoulder, and bouncing down the path toward the fish pool. "We'll see about that!" Wa kicked and thrashed like a bird caught in a net.

"Sack of rice, sack of rice, what will you pay for this sack of rice?" Xigi sang. He stopped and turned around. "On the way back, we are going to check on my traps, too, Kia, to see if we can bring Mother a squirrel or bird to cook. Want to come?"

"Maybe next time," Kia said. "Mother and I are going to see Yer's baby."

Wa wrinkled her nose. "No, babies can't do anything, and they smell like pigs. I would rather see the fish leap to get our corn."

Kia would have liked to have gone, since Xigi rarely invited her, or anyone else for that matter, to go with him. After he had been reminded to do his chores, he usually slipped away by himself, clutching his precious wrinkled tablet of paper as if it were a bar of silver, the gnawed pencil stub he was never without poking out from behind his ear. Kia's mother had found the yellowed tablet at the market, and it was Xigi's most treasured possession. Kia knew Xigi would rather talk with his pencil than with his mouth. Grandmother had once remarked that having a conversation with Xigi was like try-ing to spot a nest of ducklings at the river's edge from the mountaintop.

Kia did not think anyone had eyes that sharp. "How could anyone do that, Grandfather?" she had asked. "The mother duck makes sure no one can find the nest."

"You're right, Little Cricket. When the ducklings are ready to leave the nest they will show themselves, just as Xigi speaks when he has something to say." Kia had watched as Grandfather patted her grandmother's knee. Grandmother had continued working on the basket she was making, but her eyes met Grandfather's for a brief moment before they again slid downward.

"Where is Xigi going?" her mother asked as he and Wa disappeared into the trees.

"He's taking Wa to feed the fish," Kia replied, picking up the roll of papers Xigi had left lying on the ground. There were pictures of mountains veiled in mist and fat water buffalo browsing at the river's edge. Kia's favorite was the picture of a man playing a flute as the villagers were walking to their fields. Xigi had even drawn birds in the trees and insects half-hidden in the grass, as well as bees hovering above the flowers.

Kia's mother looked over her shoulder at Xigi's drawings. "He draws well, doesn't he?"

"When I look at Xigi's pictures, I am glad Xigi doesn't talk as much as other boys," Kia replied. I would rather look at his pictures and hear what they say. Xigi says pictures say different things to different people."

Her mother flipped through the drawings. "I think if Xigi could, he'd live in the world he imagines inside his head. Sometimes he forgets how much work there is to do." She handed the drawings to Kia, who rolled them up and placed them on Xigi's mat in the hut.

Her mother plopped Kia's straw hat on her head, and they started walking to the other end of the village where Kia's aunt Yer lived.

Kia squinted up at her mother through the glinting sun. "I think he doesn't forget. I think he just doesn't want to do it."

Her mother laughed. "I think you are right, and that's why we have to keep Xigi's head out of the clouds."

When they reached Aunt Yer's house, she was sitting outside holding her new little boy. As they approached, Aunt Yer placed the baby on a stack of blankets on the ground, and she and Kia's mother went into the hut, leaving Kia alone with the baby.

Kia knew not to fuss over a new baby or to touch his head, because the evil one would descend upon the child and steal his spirit, which would make him very sick or could even make him die. It was best to act as though new babies were common as mice in a cornfield. Aunt Yer's baby wore a lovely embroidered hat to help keep his spirit safe.

Kia pretended not to look at the little one, and although her head was turned away from him, her eyes slid over and peeked at his face. It was red as a hot pepper from the heat. She admired the baby's simple silver necklace, which warned the spirits he was not a slave, but that he belonged to a family. Kia's and Xigi's birth necklaces were kept safe in a small basket next to her mother's mat. When Kia looked at it, it was hard to believe her neck had ever been so small. Her father had made them for her and Xigi. Sometimes on long rainy days she would take them out and slip them over her wrists and push them up her arms, enjoying their cool sheen in the dimness of the hut.

After a time, Kia's eyes started to ache

from looking so far to the side, so she turned her head toward the baby, just enough to see the baby's tiny pink flowerbud mouth. His bottom lip quivered in his sleep. Every few minutes he gave a little squeak and swiveled his head from side to side. Then he grunted and sucked on his fist, which was no bigger than the smallest rice ball. Without warning, the little mouth curved down like a bent reed in the wind, and a quivering wail cut the air. Kia watched in alarm as the infant flailed his short arms and got even redder in the face.

Aunt Yer, who already had three children, came calmly and scooped her crying baby up. She held him in the air and sniffed him. Kia thought this was a funny thing to do, but Aunt Yer knew all about babies and what made them cry, so Kia sniffed the baby too. Pinching her nose, Kia decided Wa knew more about babies than she did. They did smell like little pigs!

3

Kia did not think again about the war that she and Aunt Zoua had talked about until it was time to harvest the rice. She was at the market with her mother and grandmother, helping to set out their brooms and baskets to sell, when she heard a stranger talking to two village men about soldiers who had come to his village. The stranger walked with a limp and his hands shook so badly as he talked that he finally stuffed them in his pockets.

"I tell you, this war that came to my village

will soon come here, and it will eventually destroy our whole country. Many men in my village joined the Royal Lao Army and are being trained by the Americans to fight the Communists and help keep Laos free." The man lowered his voice and stepped closer to the two men. "Those that were left, husbands and fathers, even some boys, were tied up and forced to go with these Communist soldiers of North Vietnam, who want to tell us how to live." The man slapped his bad leg. "If it weren't for this leg, they would have taken me too. Soon there will be no safe place for us."

The man had his back to her, so Kia could not see his face, but she could hear the sadness in the man's voice. She watched the three men walk away, weaving through the crowd of people carrying squawking chickens, woven mats, and cooking pots.

As she watched people bartering for the brooms and baskets, she thought back to Aunt Zoua, asking Grandfather to make the war go away. Kia wondered if he had remembered this or if he had been so busy helping others that he had forgotten.

After eating the evening meal, Kia waited anxiously for Grandfather to return from visiting with the elders of the village. Her heart was full of questions she didn't know how to ask. Xigi had disappeared into the dusk with his pencil and tablet while her mother and grandmother silently cleaned the dishes. Her father was helping to clear small trees and shrubs at the forest's edge to prepare it for planting next year. The red sun had dropped behind a mountain and the birds were calming down for the night when at last Grandfather returned home. She leaped to her feet as she saw him approach, and the words tumbled out of her.

"Grandfather, at the market today, I heard a man say the war had come to his village and that it was going to come to ours too, and that men were being taken and we wouldn't be safe anymore, but that the Americans are helping us." She squeezed his hand and searched his tired face, hoping he would tell her there was nothing to worry about. "Did you ask the spirits to make the war go away as Aunt Zoua asked?"

He drew her inside the hut, where her

mother and grandmother were stitching a new skirt for Kia to wear during the New Year celebration. Grandfather sat down and waited for them to lay their work aside.

"I have spoken to the man at the market who told of the war coming to his village." He looked at Kia. "What you heard is true. The Americans are giving us guns to help us defend ourselves so the Communists cannot take over Laos. General Vang Pao needs men to fight the Communists."

Xigi stepped silently into the hut and sat beside Kia.

"I do not understand all that is happening," Grandfather continued, "but the Americans say that if the Communists win this war, they will take our homes and make us their slaves."

Kia thought she had never heard such silence, even when she woke in the middle of the night and everyone else in the village was sleeping.

Abruptly, Xigi stood up, chin thrust out, his voice loud and harsh as a crow's. "I will go fight these Communists. No one will make me a slave."

Grandfather pushed himself to his feet and placed a hand on Xigi's shoulder. "Tonight is not the time to decide these matters. We will speak of it again in the morning."

Kia heard her father return after she had gone to bed. She could hear the low murmur of their voices as he and Grandfather talked outside the door of the hut. Her body ached with tiredness and a fear she had never before felt. What is war, she kept asking herself, and how can it mean we will not be safe here anymore?

She felt she had just dozed off when she was jarred awake by her mother, who yanked her firmly by the arm. She cracked open eyes that felt small and gritty.

"Kia, get up! Put some clothes on," her mother whispered roughly, pulling a skirt and blouse on over her own nightclothes. Kia looked over at Xigi, who was already dressed, standing in the doorway, face bathed by a wavering red brightness. Hastily, she tugged on the skimpy dress she had worn yesterday. Her heart was pounding frantically, her hands shaking as badly as the man with the limp at the market.

In the night stillness, a man's deep voice shouted, "Everyone out of your houses! Now! Come quickly or we will drag you out!"

Clutching one another, Kia, Xigi, and their mother joined her grandparents, her father, and the other villagers standing on the hard-packed dirt paths, feet stumbling in the torchlight, like a herd of nervous cows.

One soldier, who was the leader and had a jagged crimson scar that ran crookedly from his ear to his chin, kicked a sick old woman huddled on the ground. She rolled in the dirt and cradled her white head in her arms.

"Get up, you lazy *meo*!" he screamed at her. "You act like this land belongs to you! Nothing belongs to you, do you understand? Nothing! You have no right to anything here!"

Grandfather had told Kia that to be called a *meo* was to be called a barbarian. Even the roughest of the village boys knew better than to call anyone such a terrible name, or they would suffer a whipping. Horror-stricken, everyone stood frozen until Kia's father helped the sobbing old woman to her feet and led her to stand next to Kia's mother.

"Men over the age of fifteen form a line over here!" the man with the scar yelled, gesturing to the side of the path. "The rest of you, stand over there!" As the men looked from one to the other in shock and confusion, the soldier roughly prodded them with the barrel of his rifle. "Now! Move! Are you all deaf as well as stupid?"

As the men lined up shoulder to shoulder, a woman began to wail, covering her mouth with her hand. "Quiet!" shouted the soldier, "or I will not just take them to fight, I will shoot them!" The woman buried her face against the shoulder of an older woman and her cries were muffled.

Once the captured men, Kia's father among them, were tied up, hands behind their backs, the soldiers made the women cook large amounts of food for them to take on their journey. Kia's mother was forced to kill her speckled chicken because the soldiers demanded more than rice and corn to eat. Even the ancient rust-colored cow, whose hip bones jutted out like wings, was slaughtered.

Just before dawn the Communists amused themselves by shooting at the legs and feet of the women, pretending to make them dance. The young soldiers laughed and yelled, "Look at the *meo*s dance! They are not lazy now!" Tears rolled down Kia's face as she watched her old grandmother jump heavily from foot to foot. Bullets zinged off the hard-packed ground, and every so often a woman moaned and fell, clutching a bleeding leg or foot.

Kia and her cousins watched in terror when a couple of the village men who refused to go with the soldiers were shot and their huts burned. The flaming embers coasted and settled to earth as black ash. Women cried out in grief; children sat, stunned, in the dirt. The bamboo and thatch burned very quickly, and piercing screams cut through the heavy night air as mothers tried to save their meager belongings.

"Just do as they say," Kia's father whispered to her as he was prodded past her. A soldier not much older than Xigi, who smelled like rotting meat, shoved her father to the end of the line of men. Kia was too afraid to think of doing anything else. Kia's mother made a move to follow her husband, but another soldier shoved her backward with the butt of his rifle.

The soldiers and their captives shuffled off toward the river. The villagers left behind watched them go in silence. Kia kept her eyes on her father as the line of men snaked down the mountain trail. Suddenly, she saw him stop and savagely kick the knee of the soldier who walked by his side. The man dropped to the ground and groaned in pain. Kia's father melted into the dense green jungle of the mountainside and was swallowed up by bushes and thick vines.

The angry soldier struggled to his feet and started after her father, but the man with the scar on his cheek said to let him go. "One less will not matter. The ones who are left will have to fight harder to make up for the one that ran away." And with a cruel grin, he and the other soldiers led Kia's uncles and neighbors away, guns pointing at their heads.

As the tramp of the soldiers faded, some of the women ran to get the buckets of water that stood outside their houses to douse the burning huts. But the buckets of water could not save them, so the women dumped water on the huts nearest those burning, so that they would not catch fire too. Kia was glad the night was still, with barely a leaf moving on the trees, or the whole village might have gone up in flames.

It was nearly dawn when the women, children, and old men stumbled back into their homes. The families whose huts had burned stayed with those who had extra room, now that their men were gone.

As Kia lay on her mat in the gray light, listening to the hushed cries of children, she wondered if her father was safe and would come back home, now that the soldiers had left. What would they do without him? Would he return when the war was over? Who would harvest the ripening crops, with only the women and children in the village? She shifted onto her side and closed her eyes. Then she placed her fingertips over her lids, hoping the blackness would bring sleep.

4

The morning after the Communist soldiers had terrorized the village, Kia woke feeling as though she were trying to breathe underwater. The sun had risen hours before, and she couldn't remember why she was still in bed or why she couldn't seem to catch her breath. She lay listening to the familiar birdsong and monkey chatter, but the heaviness in her heart was like the charcoal storm cloud that during the rainy months rested on the great mountain she could see from the door of the hut.

Gradually, she remembered the cruel soldiers and how they had made the old woman weep. The air was thick from the smoldering huts. Worst of all, her father was gone, as were her uncles and most of the fathers of the friends she had known all her life.

For the first time in her memory, she rose before her mother. She went into the kitchen area and saw that the cooking fire was cold and the bag of rice that had been knocked over during last night's confusion still lay sprawled on the floor. She swept it up as best she could, putting the rice in a basket to be washed later in the river.

Xigi must have woken and left the hut earlier, as he was nowhere to be found. Kia peeked in at her mother, who was lying on her back, mouth loose, softly snoring, a worried crease between her closed eyes. It was rare that she saw her mother lying so still. She wondered what her mother thought about. If you were grown up and had children of your own, did you stop thinking about skipping a smooth stone across the river more times than anyone? Did you still marvel at how the moon kept getting bigger and bigger, then smaller and smaller day after day until it disappeared completely? She looked at her mother's hands, dented and rough, spotted with brown. It seemed to Kia that her mother's hands were always moving, sewing, cutting vegetables, or pulling weeds. Had they ever been small and grasping and soft like Aunt Yer's baby? She wished she could hold her mother's hands and tell her everything would be all right.

Grandmother was curled in a ball at the edge of the mat, head nearly touching her knees. Grandfather lay stiffly, his hands clenched on his chest. Father was their youngest son, the one who teased them and made them smile. Grandmother said he was a man with the heart of a child. Kia wished they were lying closer together so their worrying could be shared. Watching them sleep was like eavesdropping on their grief, so she tip-toed away, started the fire, and put water on to boil some rice.

It was late morning by the time the villagers started to gather outside to talk about what had happened. Most were still in shock and only looked at one another without speaking, eyes blank. Grandfather went to join the elders of the village to discuss what should be done next. Kia longed to go with him, but she knew her place was with her mother and grandmother. When he returned, he would tell them what he wanted them to know.

Kia was outside beating the dust from the bed mats when Xigi came back. For once he did not have his pencil stuck behind his ear or his roll of drawing paper. "The soldiers stomped through the vegetable gardens and took most of the village's chickens and pigs when they left," he said grimly. "We'll be fortunate if we harvest enough to get us through the rainy season."

Struggling to find something good about this terrible morning, Kia said, "Maybe father got away and is hiding in the jungle until the soldiers are far away. Then he will come back and help us plant again."

Xigi shook his head impatiently. "It's too late to replant most things." He looked solemnly at Kia. "Besides, I don't believe he got away."

"But I heard the man with the scar say it

wasn't worth the time to search for just one man."

"Do you think that after the way they treated that old woman they would let father disobey them and just walk away?" Stuffing some cold rice in his mouth, Xigi left to talk to the other boys, who were huddled together.

Watching him go, Kia felt a warm hand slip into hers. Little Wa wrapped her arms around Kia's legs. "Those men took my father," she whimpered, tears muddying her cheeks. "Why did they take him? Don't they know he lives here with me?"

Kia combed her fingers through the little girl's matted hair. "I don't know why they took him, Wa, but I think he'll be home soon."

"Before I go to bed?" Wa asked, rubbing an arm across her face.

Knowing what she said was a lie, but needing to believe it as much as the child, Kia replied, "Yes, Wa, I think he might be home by that time."

The little girl studied Kia's face for a long while, then reached up and kissed Kia on the cheek. Tears flooded Kia's eyes as she watched Wa walk over to a group of whispering children and squat down beside them.

That afternoon the women and the older children went down to the gardens to see how badly they were damaged. Xigi was right: much had been trampled. Many of the maturing plants had been yanked up and tossed away. Some of the rows were demolished so completely, Kia thought the soldiers must have dragged their feet deliberately through the garden as they walked. She couldn't understand why those men hated them enough to do this. The women carefully tucked the less damaged plants back into the damp earth and prayed to the spirits to help them grow. Kia and her cousins carried bucket after bucket of water from the river to help them take root again.

At least the fish pool had not been disturbed. She and Xigi stood together at the edge watching the hungry fish froth up the brown water, snapping up the last of the corn they tossed. On the way down the mountain, Kia had quietly searched for any sign that their father might be hiding in the jungle. She didn't care what Xigi said—their father was very clever and had probably escaped the soldiers and was waiting to come out until he was sure it was safe.

On the way back from the fish pool, Xigi checked his traps to see if he had caught anything. Since the soldiers had taken nearly all the animals from the village, meat would be scarce. But the traps were empty.

That evening, the two men whom the soldiers had shot were buried. Grandfather took out his *qeej*, the bamboo pipes. Usually, Kia enjoyed the mournful sound from the long, curved poles of bamboo that echoed off the mountain as he blew into them. Sometimes he played them for the New Year celebration, and boys would dance for the whole village. She loved celebrating the New Year, with its laughter, games, and good food.

But tonight, Grandfather told her, the bamboo pipes would be played for the men who had died. "The music will guide their spirits to their ancestors," he said. "This night our hearts are heavy because we have lost two good men."

Kia leaned against a tree and listened to the haunting music. It's strange, she thought, that this instrument could play such joyful, dancing tunes, yet tonight it made her feel as if she would never again feel happy. Her grandfather said the *qeej* played the music of the heart. Grandfather's words made Kia think about Xigi and how his drawings spoke of the things in his heart.

The wives of the two dead men sobbed while their children stared with solemn eyes at the two long mounds of dirt that covered their fathers. Kia had seen people buried before, but they had died of old age, sickness, or injuries. She had never before seen one man kill another, although she had heard stories of such things. But she had thought they were fables like the ones her grandfather told her. She wondered if the soldiers would have been so brave if they had not had guns.

Kia was afraid to sleep that night, even though Grandfather said the soldiers would not come back, because they had already taken everything from the villagers. She lay without moving, waiting for a flaming torch held by a soldier with a crimson scar to light up the night. She didn't remember falling asleep. When she awoke and tried to focus her tired eyes, her heart thumped like the hind legs of a rabbit, because a rosy glow bathed the doorway. But it was only the rising sun, and Kia wondered how this morning could begin like other mornings when her world seemed so broken.

5

With so many of the crops destroyed by the soldiers, there was little weeding to be done as the plants finished maturing. Usually, the women and children spent long, hot hours in the sun pulling the rapidly growing weeds. Since the soldiers had come, the empty days stretched into weeks with nothing to look forward to. The older boys amused the children by carving tops from wood for them to play with. Even the very littlest child learned that with a flick of his fingers the top would spin dizzily on the hard-packed dirt.

The women spent hours working on their *pa ndaus*. For Kia, looking at the colorful story cloths her mother and grandmother were embroidering was like having them tell her a story without words.

Her grandmother's *pa ndau* told of a village Kia had never seen, the place where her grandmother had been born. A sky full of stars shone above a village like the one in which she lived. There were scenes of men clearing trees from a field and of that field being planted with hemp seeds, from which thread came. Kia could see by the pictures her grandmother had embroidered that after the hemp was harvested, it was dried and stripped from the plant; then it was wound and spun into thread by twisting it onto big wheels. Finally, the thread was woven on the loom and cut into fabric for clothing. Grandmother said, when she was a girl this was how all her clothes were made, not like now, when you could buy clothes already made at the market.

Grandmother said Kia was nearly old enough to begin her own *pa ndau*, but Kia preferred to play games with her cousins. Kia's favorite game was finding a long, flat stick and a round, smooth stone and tying the two together with a piece of string. The trickiest part was tying the string tightly around the stone so it wouldn't slip off. The winner of the game was the one who, by flinging the stick forward, landed the stone on the stick the most times. One time when Kia was winning nearly every game, her cousin Kao grabbed Kia's stick and broke it over her knee and tossed it into the brush. Kia had searched for the perfect stick for hours and was so angry, she started to cry and ran into the hut.

When Kia had seen Kao in the fields the next afternoon, Kao poked Kia's thin arm and said Kia was so little she should still be home riding on her mother's back in a baby carrier. Kia had turned and slapped Kao, who was older and bigger. Astonished at what she had done, Kia rushed home. She cried until she hiccupped, not because she was ashamed of what she had done, but because by slapping her cousin she had disappointed Grandfather.

"One must not act out of anger," Grandfather had chided. "Like a wave in the ocean, anger quickly comes and goes."

Between hiccups Kia had sobbed, "But, Grandfather, she called me a b-b-baby!"

Grandfather remained unmoved. "What someone says to you is not important. How you act afterward is what counts." He sat Kia on his lap. "You don't want to act like the bear who found a fallen tree in which a swarm of bees had stored their honey, do you?"

"What did the bear do?"

"Well, the bear began to nose around the tree, when the swarm came home. Right away they knew he was after their honey, so a bee flew at him, stung him sharply, and disappeared into the hollow log.

"The bear lost his temper in an instant and started clawing at the log to destroy the entire nest. But, can you guess what happened? The whole swarm flew out after the bear, who was only able to save himself by diving into a pool of water." He wiped Kia's nose. "You don't want to have a nasty temper like the bear, do you? It is always better to suffer one injury quietly than to provoke a hundred by flying into a rage."

One overcast morning when Grandfather and Kia were searching for herbs, they stopped to visit Aunt Zoua. They had brought her some melons and peppers from the few plants in the garden that had produced. Aunt Zoua sat outside her hut in the same place where Kia had last seen her, as if she had turned to stone.

"Is it true," she said, greeting them, "that the Communists came to the village and all the men are gone? Including Xiong?" Xiong was Kia's father. The old woman barely turned her head toward them.

Grandfather took off his hat and placed it on his knees. Even though the day was cloudy, he never went anywhere without it. Then he scrubbed his eyes with his knuckles. "It is true. Xiong fled to the jungle, but it is doubtful he got away."

This was the first Kia had heard him speak of her father. So Grandfather, like Xigi, did not think Father had escaped the soldiers. She knew they were wrong. She wanted to scream that he had gotten away, she knew he had, because he was clever and good and she missed him so much! But, of course, she would never raise her voice to Grandfather this way. So, instead, she gathered the peppers and melons into Aunt Zoua's hut and placed them next to her bag of rice, where she would be sure to find them.

When Kia came out and sat beside her, the old woman took her hand and gently patted it.

"Your father was as playful as a river otter when he was a child," she told Kia. Her hardened gums gleamed as she grinned, remembering Xiong as a little boy. "He thought there was nothing more fun in the world than hiding when it was bedtime. One time he crawled into one of the big baskets your grandmother made, and we never would have found him if he hadn't sneezed so that the basket tipped over and he came rolling out, grinning from ear to ear."

Kia couldn't imagine her father as young as Wa. But Grandfather must have remembered his young son doing this, because a smile softened his thin lips and the crinkles around his eyes deepened with pleasure.

"What will happen now?" Aunt Zoua asked. "Will they leave us alone to mourn our sons and husbands or will they steal our souls, too?"

Grandfather stood up and put his hat on. "We must wait to see what needs to be done. If we help the Americans fight these Communists who want to ruin our country, they have said they will help us."

Sighing and struggling to her feet, Aunt Zoua steadied herself by reaching for Grandfather's arm. "I think I have lived too long," she said, turning toward her hut. "For years our people have moved from place to place to find a home where we can live in peace and love our families. I am no longer sure there is such a place." Kia watched the frail old woman totter into her hut, back rounded and head low, like a turtle, and she wondered how it felt to live too long.

"How does Aunt Zoua know she's lived too long, Grandfather?" she asked on their way home. "Does she mean she wants to die?"

Grandfather gave Kia his basket of herbs to carry. "Sometimes, Little Cricket, when you see things happen that are so hurtful, your heart shrivels within you like a lemon left to dry in the sun. The time comes when you are too tired to fight for what's right any longer."

Fear ran up Kia's spine and settled at the back of her neck. "You are not too tired to fight for what's right, are you, Grandfather?"

"You think I am as old as Aunt Zoua?" teased Grandfather, eyebrows raised. "Come here, then, let me lean on you since I am so old, I cannot walk by myself." He pulled Kia toward him and leaned heavily on her narrow shoulder. Kia slid from under his arm, laughed, and scampered down the path.

"Be careful of the herbs!" called Grandfather. "Or the rest of your day will be spent looking for more."

As the days wore on, the women and children gathered what was left of the harvest. The vegetables were scant and the rice was not as plentiful as in other years, but they were grateful for what they had. Kia's mother taught her how to spread the rice on a large woven bamboo mat in the yard to dry it so it would last until the next harvest.

One afternoon, as Kia was hauling water from the river for her mother to wash clothes, she heard a rooster crow. She followed the sound into the forest and discovered the rooster scratching at a fallen log, searching for bugs. She crept up behind him, grabbed his feet, and carried him proudly home to her mother. That night, for the first time in over a week, the family had meat to eat with their vegetables.

Xigi and the older boys started spending days at the edge of the forest trying to finish clearing the land the men had begun. It was hot, tiring work and the women talked among themselves that it was too much for young boys to do by themselves, but they let them continue because it gave the boys something else to think about instead of the war.

Gradually, the women and children settled into a rhythm, and that brought a certain comfort. Kia still thought of her father every day, but now, like Grandfather and Xigi, she did not think he had gotten away from the soldiers, or he would have come home. Now and then, Hmong soldiers would come by and tell of fierce battles in the valleys where Hmong troops were helping the Americans battle the Communists. The soldiers looked much too young to have seen the horrors they described. The women would try to shoo the children away when the soldiers talked about the war, but if they stayed still as stones, the women, in their eagerness to hear about their loved ones, would forget they were there. Sometimes Kia was afraid to hear of the men getting shot and left to die by themselves far from home, so she crept into the hut to sit and look at Xigi's drawings.

Some evenings, Xigi, after spending long days under the blistering sun with little food to fill his belly, would yell and threaten to run off to join the soldiers fighting the Communists. Kia's mother would hold her head in her hands and begin to cry and wail, "No! I have lost a husband and two brothers. I cannot lose a son too!" Although Xigi was not yet eleven, Kia had heard soldiers speak of boys not much older joining the war.

Kia wondered if Xigi's outbursts were the reason Grandfather finally left to help the Americans. If he left, Xigi would feel obligated to stay home to help with the work, like the other boys in the village.

It was a black, moonless night when Grandfather spoke of his intentions. "I know I am too old to fight, but I know these mountains better than anyone. I have walked them my whole life. The Americans do not know where the enemy hides. But I do. I can help them find their camps. A group of American and Hmong soldiers is camped not far from here. I will join them.

"We each have a duty," he said, looking hard at Xigi. "Yours is to stay and help your mother and grandmother. The women cannot be left on their own. You must do as your father would want you to do." Xigi knew better than to argue with Grandfather, but Kia could tell by the way Xigi's jaw tightened and the muscles in his cheek twitched that he was burning inside with unspoken words of anger.

The morning Grandfather left was unbearably hot, the sun a white ball baking the mountaintop. Grandmother was devastated that he was leaving and was resting in the hut, Kia's mother cooling her forehead with damp cloths. Kia and Xigi both watched as the old man made his way down the steep path, his knife swinging at his waist, a small bundle of food tied over his shoulders. Kia looked up at Xigi, who was staring after Grandfather.

"What will happen to us if the Americans do not win the war?" asked Kia. There was a hollow ache in her chest she had never felt before. She had never been without Grandfather to talk to and explain things to her. Except for three old men, bent and crippled, Xigi was the oldest male left in the village now.

In an even tone, he replied, "Some say we will all be hunted down and killed by the Communists. But the Americans will not let that happen. When they see how men like Father and Grandfather fight for them, they will take care of us."

"I am glad you are still here, Xigi," said Kia softly. "Until Father and Grandfather come back we must all stay together." And because she knew Xigi still felt bad about being left behind, she added, "I will try to help you all I can even though there's much I can't do."

His eyes crinkled up with sudden laughter, and with a snort Xigi replied, "Living among all these women is worse than fighting the Communists. Father and Grandfather are the lucky ones." Kia did not believe what Xigi said and she did not think he believed it either, but she knew it made him feel like a man to say so.

The rains were light that year, and Kia's grandmother said she had never seen a spring so dry. The stream where the children once caught fish with their bare hands was nothing but a dusty ravine. Xigi's fish pool was nearly dried up. The few fish that were left, Xigi dried and stored. Kia and the women had to go far down the valley to find water and they hauled bucket after bucket up the rocky path. At sunset each day Kia could see and smell fires burning in the distance. Drifting black smoke and ash made her throat sore and her nose itch. At night under the bright stars, the rattle of gunfire and rumble of planes lulled her to restless sleep.

During the day children drew pictures in the fine, gray dust outside their huts. The few old men and even the women moved like ghosts around the village. To Kia, it seemed as if the burning sun had dried up not only the water but the laughter as well. As the months dragged by, more and more villagers packed up their belongings to escape the sounds of war that came nearer and nearer. Whenever Kia's mother talked about leaving, Kia's grandmother wouldn't hear of it until her husband returned.

On an afternoon so hot it hurt to breathe, Kia and her cousins were scattering a few cupfuls of precious water over the parched vegetable garden when she spotted an old man limping up the mountainside with the help of a sturdy stick. His ragged clothes and long beard fluttered in the hot wind. As though he could feel someone watching him, he stopped to look up at her, squinting painfully against the white glare of the sun. With a shout of joy, Kia tumbled down the hillside and threw herself at the thin, tattered man that was her grandfather.

He was very sick, and for days he lay on his

mat and slept, barely waking to take the broth Grandmother fussed at him to drink. Finally, he began to talk about how he and many other Hmong men helped injured American pilots who had been shot down by the North Vietnamese.

"At first, the Americans were afraid of us. They thought we were the enemy. At last they understood we wanted to help them. We kept them hidden until they were well again. We bandaged their wounds, scouted for them, fed them, bathed them, until they could join their fellow soldiers. Some were not much older than Xigi and would cry out in the night for their mothers." Closing his eyes, he whispered, "War causes so much pain." His eyelids were as transparent as rice paper.

When he was stronger, Grandfather sat in the shade of the hut. He did not talk and joke with the village children as he used to do or go for long walks gathering herbs. Oftentimes, he would put on his red shaman's veil and tiny finger bells and ask the spirits of the air to end this horrible war that was killing so many.

6

When the Americans began dropping bombs on Communist camps near Kia's village, Grandfather said they, too, must leave. At last, he felt strong enough to make the long journey.

Kia was almost relieved to leave the village, because nearly everyone had already gone, and she did not like looking at the abandoned huts that had been home to her laughing, fun-loving cousins. Only Aunt Zoua remained. She said an old woman like herself would only be a nuisance on a long journey. She would die where she had lived. When they brought her some of the last of their vegetables, she wrapped her thin arms around Kia and laid her wrinkled cheek against her glossy black hair. Kia prayed silently for Aunt Zoua, and because she was afraid for the old woman, she sobbed all the way down the mountain.

Grandmother brought out some large baskets she had made and placed them in the middle of the hut. "I never thought we would use these to move from our home," she sighed.

"Where will we go, Grandfather? Will we be safer in another village?" Kia could not imagine living anywhere other than this mountaintop she knew almost as well as Grandfather.

"We must prepare for a long journey, Little Cricket. No place is safe in Laos anymore. We must find our way to Thailand, across the great river, where many of our people are being taken care of." The old man stopped, and his voice cracked as he continued. "Then, because we fought on the side of the United States, we may be able to go to America to live. There, we will be safe."

Kia watched carefully as her mother wrapped all the different vegetable seeds in pieces of silk to be saved for the next planting. Every year she did this so they would always have seeds to plant and food to eat.

Kia thought much about America as she helped her mother pack their few belongings. Kia said the word *America* to herself many times, but it meant nothing. It was just a foreign word without meaning.

"Do you think Father will be able to find us after we leave?" Soon it would be a year since the Communist soldiers had come, and no one had heard anything about the men from their village.

Her mother stopped folding a blanket and sat down on a mat. "I think if he is meant to find us, he will find us." She picked at a small hole in the fabric.

Chewing on her lip, Kia suggested, "Maybe if we leave one of Grandmother's empty baskets he will know we are safe, but had to leave. Then he will know to look for us."

Like most of the people in the village, Kia's family couldn't read or write.

Kia's mother smiled slightly for the first time in days. "That is a fine idea. We will do just that, Kia."

Kia placed a bag of rice in the bottom of a basket next to a blanket. "Is America like here? Are there mountains and forests with rivers, and herbs Grandfather needs?"

Reaching for the small basket containing Kia's and Xigi's silver birth necklaces, the only thing of value the family owned, and laying it on top of the blanket to be packed, her mother replied, "First, let's worry about getting across the Mekong River. One of the Hmong soldiers told Grandfather it is a very dangerous crossing because the Communists shoot at people trying to reach Thailand. Once we have done that, then we will worry about America."

The family took only what they could carry in the baskets on their backs: a blanket, a few extra clothes, as much food as they had left, pots for cooking, jugs of water. Xigi managed to slide his drawings in between the blanket and some clothes. Kia had been afraid he would not take them with him; he had not used his tablet since

Father left. Besides the basket on his back, Grandfather would also bring the *qeej* he had learned to play when he was eleven years old.

Looking at Xigi's yellow tablet, Kia had a wonderful thought. "Xigi," she said excitedly, "maybe you could draw a picture for Father of us crossing the big river to Thailand? Then he'll know where we are!"

"Do you still think he's coming home, Kia?" Without moving, Xigi stared at her from under his dark eyebrows.

Kia was shocked. "He may not come home now, Xigi, but he will come home sometime."

Xigi started to say something else, but Grandmother said sharply, "It's a good idea, Xigi. Do as Kia suggests."

Both Xigi and Kia looked at Grandmother, who rarely talked to them this way. In answer, Xigi tore off a sheet of paper and silently began drawing.

The next morning Kia and her family left their village, their dreams and belongings in the bamboo baskets slung across their backs. An empty basket in the middle of the room with

Xigi's picture tucked inside was all that was left in the hut. Kia's throat was tight with unshed tears. She had never been farther from home than the next green mountaintop, where the villagers had grown fields of corn, and the valley between, where the rice was harvested. She did not dare look behind her, but walked steadily forward just as the old red cow that pulled the plow used to do. She did not think. She did not feel. She just kept putting one foot in front of the other.

That first day of walking was the worst. They crossed their barren fields, knowing they would never plant them again. Before the sun was high overhead, Kia's back throbbed with the weight of the basket. She was about to ask if they could stop and rest, but she glanced over at her grandmother who trudged beside her, mouth tight with determination, and held her tongue. At day's end, Kia's shoulders throbbed, and long red welts from the basket's thumping and tugging streaked down her back.

At night they tried to find sheltered areas beneath the trees to sleep. Kia worried that her grandfather wasn't getting enough sleep, because whenever she woke during the night he was sitting with his back against a tree, gazing somewhere far past their campsite.

As they walked, the bombs dropped around them, sometimes so close the ground shook. Little animals, squirrels and monkeys, darted from tree to tree above them. One time Kia thought she saw a tiger slink through the underbrush ahead of them.

The sky was almost always clouded with ash, except when a rain shower briefly cleaned the air, and they tied scarves over their mouths and noses. They had no map to tell them where they were going, so they relied on Grandfather's knowledge of the country.

They passed a few people on their way to the river. From them they learned that the war was not going as well for the Americans as they had hoped. The North Vietnamese Communists knew the land much better than they did and it was difficult for the Americans to root them out. They also learned that many Hmong had died fighting.

For weeks Kia and her family lived on

mushrooms and scratched in streambeds for crabs and crayfish. They wandered from place to place, sleeping under roofs of banana leaves that clattered in the hot wind. Once, they were forced to hide in a damp cave with three other families until the rains stopped. Lying outside the cave were dead Hmong soldiers still clutching their rusting rifles.

On one of these nights some Communist soldiers passing through put up tents just outside their cave. They cursed and yelled and shot their guns off late into the night. The families huddled silently together at the back of the cave in frigid water up to their ankles. Kia's feet were numb. To quiet a fussy baby, a frightened young mother pinched the child's nose closed so it had to breathe through its mouth and couldn't get breath to cry.

Kia didn't know how many days they had traveled, but she knew there had been two full moons since they had left their village. There was little food left and almost none to be found. Often Kia felt like crying, until she looked at her shrunken grandfather, who kept them heading toward the river without complaint simply because there was nothing else to do but to survive.

A few times they found cans that the Americans had dropped from their airplanes to help feed people trying to get to Thailand. Kia's mother opened a few with her knife, and they gratefully ate the fish inside. Once they found some packets of salt and a striped blanket, which Kia's mother packed in her basket.

One night they came upon a neglected cornfield. As they started gathering the remaining withered ears of corn, an army of great red-eyed rats dragging long skinny tails came snarling at them. Nearly crazed with hunger, Kia and her family armed themselves with heavy sticks and clubbed as many as they could. Then they skinned them and cooked them over an open fire. As she ate, numb with cold and hunger, she decided war meant hunger and pain and worry so deep even your teeth ached. War, she thought, turns people into animals.

Finally, they met up with a man from their village who was now a guerilla fighter against the

Communists. He told them Kia's father had been captured and shot by the North Vietnamese army not far from their village. He had been killed because he told them he would not fight on the side of the Communists. Kia's mother and grandmother wailed until their voices were hoarse. Kia remembered the dead soldiers outside the cave they stayed in and wondered if anyone had buried her father. In a tired but steady voice, Grandfather said, "My son died doing what he believed to be right. We must do what's right so we can live without fear."

Kia couldn't believe she would never see him again. Back in the village, the hut had never seemed like home until her father got home in the evening. He was never too tired to listen to Xigi tell about the traps he was setting, or to Kia as she explained a new game she had invented. Kia's mother had sometimes sent them to bed early so he could rest.

She wondered if her father had been afraid when he died or if, like Aunt Zoua, he had somehow known his life here was over. Sometimes it was hard for Kia to remember her father's face, so she decided to remember him as the little boy Aunt Zoua had talked about. She liked to think of him as the giggling child spilling out of the basket, laughing at his cleverness in fooling the adults.

Xigi became quieter than ever after learning of the death of his father. Kia had tried to tell him what Aunt Zoua had said, but he had retorted, "I know what he was like, Kia. I knew him longer than you did."

Kia felt as though she had been punched in the stomach. She didn't like to think that Xigi had known Father longer than she had, but, of course, it was true. He was two years older than she. Xigi probably knew many things about Father she didn't. Still, she clung to the memory of her young father and remembered him at night when she was chilled and weary.

After what seemed a lifetime, Kia and her family reached the great river, the Mekong. If they could cross the river to Thailand, they would be safe. But throughout their journey, they had been warned that many people had died trying to reach the other side. For weeks they lived in the hills overlooking the river, waiting until it was safe to cross. Kia would never forget the night cries of the wild animals as she fell asleep. In the early mornings, monkeys chattered gaily as they cavorted in the treetops, unaware of the sad and frightened people huddled beneath them. On the opposite shore a few small buildings and temple towers peeked above the trees. Then the land stretched flat as far as Kia could see. Thin water buffalo lay in the yellow mud of the river, the skin hanging loose between their ribs. Under the hot sun of day the long, lazy river did not look dangerous, but gunfire and cries of terror rang through the night.

There was no moon the night they decided to cross the river. Kia and her family used tough weeds to tie together the bamboo poles they had collected. Rags were wrapped around their feet to protect them from sharp stones and brambles. The raft was lopsided and uneven and halfway across the river the poles separated. Before she latched onto a drifting pole, Kia sucked in mouthfuls of the dirty water. Kia's grandmother could not swim and would have drowned had

Kia's mother not used her skirt to tie the terrified old woman's hands to a bamboo pole.

The strong current carried Kia far downstream until the pole became lodged in a bank and she scrambled onto firm ground. Exhausted, Kia lay in the tall weeds, basket still strapped to her shoulders. She looked back at the land that was Laos. All she could see was a dark line where the water met the shore. In front of her there were lights and harsh, muffled sounds she had never heard before. Briefly, she felt excitement, thinking of all the new things she would see. Then she thought of her father and that he was never going to see any of this, so she lay her head down in the mud and closed her eyes until she heard Grandfather's call.

Unlike many families, they had all made it safely across into Thailand. They were some of the lucky ones.

7

Several Thai policemen found Kia's family as they huddled on the shore and led them to a small shack in which to spend the night. One of the policemen told them that in the morning, only a few hours away, they would be taken to Ban Vinai, a refugee camp. They were each given a handful of cold rice before they were shown to a row of dirty, unraveling mats. Kia wondered how many other families had collapsed on them, bone tired, half-drowned, waiting to be taken somewhere else. They were so tired they didn't even take off their wet clothes or unpack their sodden baskets.

At dawn, two policemen herded Kia and her family into the backseat of a car, their baskets crammed on the floor. It was the first car Kia had ever seen. When it roared down the road a tunnel of dust spewed up behind them. She watched it fan out behind them until she started feeling sick. Once they were away from people and buildings, the driver pulled the car off the road into an overgrown weedy field and jerked to a stop.

The driver turned to Kia's grandfather and asked gruffly, "How are you going to pay for my taking you to the camp?"

"Pay? We have nothing with which to pay you." Grandfather looked bewildered.

Shaking his head and lifting a shoulder, the Thai driver replied, "That's too bad, because I can't take you to the camp for nothing. We might as well go back, then." He started to turn the wheel of the car back the way they had come.

"Wait." Grandfather leaned over and spoke to Kia's mother in a low voice. Kia, who was sitting on the other side of Xigi, couldn't hear what he said.

The driver tapped his fingers impatiently on the steering wheel.

Kia's mother stared at Grandfather in disbelief and exclaimed, "But it is all we have left!" Her eyes raced pleadingly from Grandfather back to Grandmother. Finally, she reached into her basket and pulled out the small basket containing Xigi's and Kia's beautiful silver birth necklaces. She fingered them lovingly for a moment before reluctantly handing them to Grandfather, who gave them to the driver.

Smirking, the driver dropped them in the pocket of his shirt. "This barely pays for the gas to get you there!"

Bewildered that Grandfather would so easily part with things so dear to their family, Kia felt betrayed. Why had he given them to that man who was nothing more than a thief? It would have been better to let the man take them back to the river.

She sat woodenly, looking out the window until she couldn't hold the words in any longer.

Kia was thrown sideways into Xigi as the car lurched onto the rutted road.

"Grandfather, that man cares nothing for our necklaces!" she whispered angrily, leaning across Xigi. "Father made them for us and they are all we have left of him. Why did you give them to that horrid man?"

Leaning toward her, he spoke quietly to both her and Xigi. "You are wrong, Little Cricket. You and Xigi are the most precious things left by your father. The necklaces are beautiful, but they are only things. Do you not think people are much more valuable than things? Isn't it more important that we treasure you and Xigi as your father would want?"

She looked into her grandfather's eyes. There were red pouches beneath them that had never been there before. Slowly nodding her head, she was ashamed she had not thought before she had spoken.

At first when Kia saw Ban Vinai she couldn't believe her eyes. Inside the fence, as far as she could see, there were rows of long thatched and bamboo houses and people of all ages bustling about. Boys were playing soccer; a little girl no older than Wa was getting her hair cut shorter than Xigi's. A woman with her hair held back with a red barrette was pouring water from a bucket over a child so thin Kia could count his ribs.

The driver hurried Kia's family out of the car and up to a gate in the fence, where he talked briefly with another man. This man asked Grandfather some questions, looked through a stack of papers, then motioned for them to follow him. There was so much to see, Kia didn't watch where she was going and kept tripping over Xigi, who was walking in front of her. The child the mother had been bathing was shivering and staring at them with enormous eyes.

As they walked, Grandfather spoke. "This man says no one else from our village has been placed in this camp. He said there are many other camps they may have been sent to." She wondered where the aunts and cousins that had left the village before them were. She was afraid the river had pulled them under as it had tried to pull her. She remembered hearing the gunshots at night, too, and seeing the bodies of those that had been shot lined up under the trees.

Grandfather continued. "I have told him about your father and that I helped the Americans find the North Vietnamese near the mountains of our home. He said, if we choose, we can apply to go to America because we helped fight against the Communists."

Xigi stopped so quickly, Kia crashed into him, spilling her basket of wet clothes in the dirt. "So, we are going to America?" Xigi asked in a high voice.

Without slowing down or looking at anyone, his *qeej* bumping against his hip, Grandfather replied, "If it is what we want to do."

Kia threw the wet clothes back into the basket and ran to catch up to Grandfather. She glanced at her mother and grandmother and wondered if the thought of going to America both excited and terrified them as it did her. She did not know much about America, only what she'd heard from a few traders who had been there and had returned with goods to sell at the village market.

There were so many new things for Kia to see and think about she hardly noticed they were being led to a long thatched hut with a large room for cooking and eating, and a few small bedrooms just large enough for sleeping mats. The family with whom they would share the house watched them enter, lugging their baskets. Kia counted six adults and eleven children.

Xigi was fascinated with all the new things to see. Each day he roamed the camp and studied the way the people who ran the camp talked and dressed. He shadowed the interpreters, who were able to answer his many questions. Then he would come back to the hut and report what he had learned. One afternoon he came home with some news that made Kia's grandmother and mother smile.

"We can rent a space outside the fence to plant vegetables! Then you won't have to stand in line all day to get food!"

Each day, Kia and her mother stood for hours to receive small amounts of rice, vegetables, or fish. There was never enough to eat, and

Kia's belly was always rumbling when she went to sleep at night.

"And, if we earn some money," continued Xigi with a sparkle in his eyes, "we can buy candy bars and pop!" Xigi particularly loved the gum the Thai traders sold at the market. One of the children who had lived at the camp for a long time had let him try a piece. But it all cost money, money Kia's family didn't have.

Grandfather stood and looked out the door at the number of people milling about the packed-dirt streets. Often he stood there for a long time, and Kia wondered if he was seeing past the wandering children and the bewildered adults to his beloved mountains. "And just where will we get the money to rent this land?"

Xigi smiled smugly. "I've already figured out a way. One of the boys showed me a way to sneak out through the fence at night." He looked at Grandmother. "I can get as much grass as you need to make your baskets. Then, we can sell them to get the money to rent the land."

Grandfather turned to Xigi. "And what if you get caught?"

"I won't. But Yo said even if the guards see you go, they don't care, as long as you aren't causing trouble."

Kia thought it was a daring idea and wanted to be part of it. "Can I go too, Grandfather?"

As if talking to himself, Grandfather muttered, "Who would have thought we would have to sneak out through a fence to help earn money to eat?" Kia watched Grandfather's shoulders curve forward a little more before he stepped out into the brilliant sunshine. Kia's mother spoke sharply, telling Kia she could not go.

That night Xigi was allowed to go with the other boys outside the camp. He gathered armfuls of grasses that Kia's grandmother wove into baskets. The people living in Ban Vinai were happy to buy such well-made baskets, and soon the family had enough money with which to rent a small space for a garden. As they had back in Laos, Grandfather dug the holes for the seeds and Kia, her mother, and Grandmother planted the okra, peppers, beans, and other vegetables from the seeds they had carried so far.

During the day, Xigi ran with the boys of the camp, armed with a slingshot, taking aim at anything that moved. Most boys owned a fighting rooster and large crowds watched the birds fight. Those that didn't have roosters caught large bugs with rhinoceros-like horns that could be trained to fight each other. Xigi captured a chameleon and tried to make a pet of it until it bit him on the thumb and wouldn't let go. Grandfather had to pry the reptile's mouth open with a stick.

Xigi never took his pencil and paper with him anymore. Kia had retrieved the damp drawings from his basket and laid them to dry in the sun. Some of them were badly wrinkled, but not ruined. When they had dried, Kia rolled them up again and put them away.

Kia wondered if Xigi talked to the camp boys now that he didn't talk through his drawings anymore. Sometimes when she was getting water from the big tanks that were as tall as three huts piled on top of each other, she heard him speaking to them. They always talked about the motorcycle one of the young American doctors used to get around the camp or of the cassette tapes sold at the market and the music they played.

One day Xigi left on his mat a magazine another boy had given him. Kia sat down on her mat, and even though she couldn't read a word, the pictures opened a world for her she'd never imagined. There were happy, laughing people in every picture. Sometimes they were drinking out of shimmering glasses that looked like rainbows, other times they were dressed in beautifully colored clothes that clung to their trim bodies as they walked down a street lined with unbelievably tall buildings that shut out the sun. There were pictures of cats napping on windowsills and a girl curled up on her smiling father's lap, looking at pictures in a book. The little girl wore a gold ring on her finger. Kia studied this picture for a long time. She pretended she was the pretty girl in the pink gown and ribbon in her hair, knees tucked under her chin, pointing to something in the book that made her father smile. Making sure no one else was in the hut, she tore the picture from the magazine, folded it up, and put it under her mat.

She wished she knew what the pretty girl was

pointing at that made her father smile so. Maybe every night they sat together, heads touching, and read stories with happy endings, stories where fathers didn't die and soldiers didn't shoot at old women. In bed that night, she pondered why the magazine people looked so happy. Was it because they had so much? There was gold encircling their necks, their wrists, and in their ears; clothes Kia had never before seen, colors and styles she never could have imagined; houses made of windows, filled with things she had no words to describe; pages and pages of bold, black words she couldn't understand. Their easy smiles and laughing faces planted themselves in her heart, declaring that life was nothing but a grand adventure.

Wide-eyed in the darkness, she wondered how these laughing people would act if everything they knew were ripped from them. Kia flip-flopped on her mat so much that her mother finally asked her what the matter was, why she couldn't go to sleep, and would she please lie still. So Kia lay quietly, self-pity flaring in her chest like a spark in dry brush. For the first time in her life discontentment surged through her.

She was growing old from fear and worry, anxious that tomorrow would find her with even less than she had today. The joy she had known had died along with her father. More than anything, she wanted to be like the smiling people in the magazine who were surrounded by beautiful things. She recalled the feel of her silver birth necklace, cool and smooth against her arm, and the pleasure of knowing it belonged to her. That was gone, but there were other things in the camp she had seen that she was sure would make her just as happy.

For instance, Ia, the daughter of the family they lived with, had a ring that Kia admired. It was gold and had a red stone. Ia was careful of it and only wore it when she was finished helping with the wash or working in their garden. Kia wondered what it would be like to wake up in the morning and know that you owned a beautiful ring like that and could wear it whenever you wanted.

Kia decided she would find out. Late one sultry morning when Ia was with her family bathing in the nearby lake, Kia took Ia's ring from the small box by her bed where she kept it and, wrapping it in a square piece of cloth, tucked it far underneath her mat.

Kia was in the garden when Ia, weeping, ran up to her and asked if she had seen her ring. Ia's eyes were red and swollen. Kia could feel her heart beating faster, but she continued weeding and just shook her head. Ia stood sniveling for a moment or two before she turned and walked dejectedly back to the hut.

That night, Kia made sure she stayed awake after everybody else had gone to sleep. She quietly felt under her mat for the ring wrapped in the cloth. It fit perfectly the middle finger of her right hand, just as she was sure it would. It was too dark in the hut to see the deep red stone, but she ran her fingers over and over it, feeling its smoothness. She told herself the ring was hers now, she would keep it hidden so no one would see it. She remembered the laughing women in the magazine, their ringed fingers wrapped around sparkling glasses. Now she had a ring like that, and when she got to America, she would laugh as they did because things would be different there.

8

Occasionally, during the long soft evenings, Grandfather would play his bamboo *qeej*, its wheezing notes lingering in the night air. Although it had been an awkward thing to carry for long distances, Kia was glad he had brought it. People from all over the camp would come and listen while he played.

Grandfather stroked the long curved bamboo pipes. "The young must learn to play the *qeej* so that after I am gone, they will be able to send spirits back to their ancestors."

Listening to the *qeej*, Kia feel peaceful and sad at the same time. "Will you teach Xigi how to play?"

Grandfather blew several mournful notes through the long bamboo stem before he answered. "If he wants to learn."

But Xigi and the other boys never stayed to listen to Grandfather play the *qeej*. They would form soccer teams or sometimes play against the neighboring Thai boys. Their matches were loud and competitive and lasted into the night. Sometimes Xigi would come home with extra money that he gave to his mother. When Kia asked him where he got the money, he said he sold the cigarettes he won at the rooster fights by picking the winner.

Because Kia's mother and grandmother were busy making baskets to sell to pay the rent on their land, Xigi was forced to help Kia weed the garden.

"I would rather be fighting the Communists," Xigi would growl as he yanked the stubborn weeds that grew quickly in the tropical air. "I'm old enough now. The sooner this war is over, the sooner we will get to America." They had been in the refugee camp for more than a year. Some refugees had found sponsors and had left for America even as more refugees from Laos poured in every week. Kia said nothing, hoping that if Xigi grumbled to her he would not say such things at home to upset their mother again.

With some of the extra money Xigi brought home, he and Kia began attending English lessons taught in open-sided buildings with corrugated metal roofs that were hot as flames to the touch. Since there had been no school in their village in Laos, they could not read or write in Hmong. The teacher at the camp school spoke to them in Hmong, but taught them how to write and say the English words. They had to share books with other students, but they each received a tablet and pencil to practice with at home. Kia went through the tablets so quickly, filling them with the strange letters, that the teacher laughed and said Kia would be reading Shakespeare before long. Kia had no idea who Shakespeare was, but smiled anyway, glad she made the teacher happy.

Long days of inactivity made Grand-mother's tongue sharper than usual, and she scolded so much that Kia and Xigi learned to keep away from her. Kia's mother seemed to lack energy even to cook, so it fell to Kia to prepare the scanty meals. They were given food twice a day and were luckier than some, because they had fresh vegetables from their garden.

Digging in the garden under the warm sun made Kia feel that her father was near. That was when she struggled to recall everything about him that she could, so she would never forget. She thought about the way his black eyebrows had curved like crescent moons above his eyes and how his mustache had prickled when he kissed her. He had not been a tall man, but his shoulders and arms were thick with muscle from working the fields and cutting trees. Sometimes when he came home at night he would swing Kia in circles until it looked like the trees grew sideways and the sky was an upside-down bowl. When he finally set her down, they would laugh together as her knees buckled and she crumpled dizzily to the ground.

For Kia, tending the garden became a refuge where the uncertainty and grind of everyday life evaporated like fog shrouding the river. But Kia would have gladly done without it if only Grandfather would be happy and hum, the way he had before the war.

"What will happen to us now, Grandfather?" she asked as they sat outside the hut together. "Will we stay here forever?"

Not raising his eyes from the stony ground, he replied, "I do not know. Does it make a difference?" This answer made Kia more afraid than ever, because she knew Grandfather would never have said such a thing before the war started.

After Grandfather left to walk aimlessly around the camp, her mother tried to comfort her. "He is just tired," said her mother, seeing fat tears slide down Kia's cheeks. "He is not used to doing nothing. He has always had people to make better and medicines to find. Here, the hours are empty and he feels he is not needed anymore."

"Why don't they need him? There are many sick people here." It was true. Many people were sick, but they were treated by an American doctor who traveled around the camp on the motorcycle much admired by Xigi and boys.

Kia's mother explained, "The Americans and the other people who have come here to help us do not do things the way we do. If the Americans see our people going to see a shaman instead of one of their doctors, they may not take us to America. They do not understand our ways. They think our beliefs are foolish. We must pretend to be as they are so they will accept us."

Finally, after nearly three years at the camp, Kia's family learned that a Catholic Church in Minnesota had raised money to bring them to the United States. Members of the parish of St. Mary's Church would help them find a place to live and teach them how to live in America. At first Kia's grandmother said she would not go. "Why should we go halfway around the world to live?" she demanded. "What do they have there that we need? Soon maybe the war will be over and we can return home to Laos."

Grandfather had taken his wife's hands,

held them tightly, and held her eyes with his. "Opportunity," he said softly. "Opportunity for our children, so they can grow and learn."

Afraid and angry, the old woman searched her husband's face. "What of us? I am too old to learn a new way to live. My bones are tired." Her voice cracked as she tried to pull her hands away. Grandfather only held on tighter.

"You may not be young, but you are still the most beautiful thing in the world to me." Kia had never heard her grandfather speak so tenderly. She watched as Grandmother rested her head on Grandfather's shoulder and closed her eyes.

When they found out they would soon be leaving for Minnesota, Kia and Xigi began learning English more quickly than before. They were so excited about coming to America, they made a game of who could learn English the fastest. Some of the families still in the camp had received letters from relatives in America, who said that anything in the world could be found in America.

Like most of the women in the camp, Kia's mother and grandmother did not go to the classes. Grandfather started the classes, but quickly found the new sounds difficult to say and finally refused to go at all. Instead, he shuffled around the camp, chin low, white beard bouncing on his chest, muttering to himself. When he tired of this, he began to embroider beautiful, colorful *pa ndaus* like those the women made. Grandfather's *pa ndau*s were filled with birds and animals and pictures of what their lives had been like back in Laos. There were stands of corn, ribbons of blue water, and villages like theirs with thatched huts and children playing. When Kia looked at them, the heaviness in her heart lifted, if only for a little while.

Whenever Xigi was away from Grandfather, he bragged about the motorcycle and cassette player that he would soon have.

"Just wait," he told Kia. "America has everything. We will be rich. Never again will I wear these old clothes." Making a sour face, he fingered the baggy cotton pants that were tied with rope at his waist. Kia did not know what it would be like to be rich, but it must be good, because she had never seen Xigi's black eyes shine so. They gleamed like polished river stones.

Two days before Kia and her family were to leave the refugee camp a tall, tired-looking American woman with small round glasses and blond hair spiky with sweat came to see them. A Hmong interpreter was with her. The woman carried a folder jammed with crinkled papers. She asked Grandfather what their family name was, and she began thumbing through the folder. As she was doing this, a hot gust of wind swirled through the dusty camp, sending the papers somersaulting into the air.

"Oh, my!" the woman cried in dismay, turning her back to the wind and hugging the folder tight to her body. Kia and Xigi gathered as many papers as they could find, but it was impossible to be sure they had gotten them all because the wind sailed them up and about like dried leaves from a banana tree.

"Let's see. Vang, Vang." Because the papers were so mixed up, it took her a long time to sort through them. Every few seconds she sighed as she ran a stubby finger up and down dozens of pages. "Here we are. Headed for Minnesota, due to leave in two days. Everything looks to be in order." With the back of her hand the woman wiped away a drop of sweat that was dripping off her short, pointed nose. "Three family members cleared for relocation: Meng Vang, Xigi Vang, and Kia Vang. Be ready to leave at 0700 hours on the twenty-fifth." Kia and her family waited patiently while the interpreter told them what the woman had said.

"There is some mistake," Grandfather told the interpreter. "There are five of us going, not three." When the interpreter had finished speaking, the woman checked the sheet again. She ran a hand through her short hair so that it stood straight up from her forehead.

"I only have three names here. I'm sorry, but I'm not authorized to make any changes."

Grandfather spoke clearly and patiently to the interpreter, never taking his eyes off the American woman's face. "We cannot break apart our family. We must stay together. Perhaps you can speak to the officer in charge about this mistake."

The woman crammed the papers back into the folder and peered at Grandfather over the tops of her glasses. Kia saw that her brown eyes were tired and bloodshot. "Mr. Vang, I understand your problem, but emigration takes months and months of planning. I can't just write down five people instead of three. I will see what I can do, but I can't promise you anything. I'm afraid the two remaining family members will have to stay until plans can be made to have them join you." Seeing that Grandfather was not satisfied with her answer, she added, "I'll speak to my superior officer. You can come with me if you'd like."

Kia watched as Grandfather followed the woman to the barracks where the man in charge of emigration had his office. Kia thought he looked very small beside the tall woman, who took one long stride for every two steps Grandfather took. Almost immediately Grandfather returned. "It is no use. The man in charge has left for ten days. The woman says if Xigi, Kia, and I do not leave as planned it could be months, even years before we are cleared to leave again. She says the church who is helping pay for us will just choose another family if we do not come." Grandfather looked steadily at Kia's grandmother, who was slowly nodding her head.

"She is right," said Kia's grandmother. "We cannot keep Xigi and Kia here any longer. It is not good for them to stay here. We must think of the children. Dia and I will wait."

"But, Grandfather!" exclaimed Kia. "The papers with Mother's and Grandmother's names on them must have blown away! Xigi and I will go look until we find them. Then we will all be able to go together." Kia started to run off, but Grandfather gently touched her shoulder.

"You may look, Little Cricket, but do not be disappointed if they are not found. They may not have been there to begin with."

Kia and Xigi searched the camp for hours, but never found any more papers. That evening, the blond woman and the interpreter came to Kia's hut. The woman said a mistake had been made in entering the family name. Grandmother and Kia's mother had mistakenly been entered under the name of Yang, instead of Vang. She was terribly sorry, but felt it best if the other three family members went on ahead until arrangements were made with the church for the other two to join them.

That evening after they had eaten, Kia's mother helped them pack the baskets that would carry their belongings to America. They had little more now than they had when they had first come to the refugee camp, but both Xigi and Kia did have two extra sets of clothes and a pair of sandals, since they had been told it was cold in Minnesota. Kia was careful to keep the ring she had taken from Ia hidden in the pocket of an extra pair of pants.

Kia had never spent a day apart from her mother, and the thought of leaving her behind at the camp terrified her. "We will be fine," her mother assured her. "We will continue making and selling baskets as fine as this one, and soon we will be with you again." She brushed the hair back from Kia's forehead. "You must promise me one thing." She handed Kia a packet. "These are our vegetable seeds from the plants in Laos and now here. The light-haired woman told us the church made arrangements for you to have some land not far from where you will live." Her voice quivered, and she stopped for a moment before continuing. "Plant these seeds so you will always have a garden to care for. I have seen how you lose your worries, Kia, when you take care of a garden." She placed her hands on either side of Kia's face. "Remember, we are Hmong, no matter where we live. And care for Grandfather. He is not as young as you and Xigi. You will make a new life there. His world is in Laos. You must help him."

When the bus carrying Grandfather, Xigi, and Kia pulled away from the camp to the place where the plane waited, Kia's mother had run alongside, clutching Kia's hand until she could no longer keep up. Kia kept her eyes on her mother until she was lost in the crowd. There had been so many times over the past years that she had been frightened, but this time, looking at Grandfather sitting stiff and wooden, and Xigi, thumbing nervously through a new magazine, she felt her heart was as heavy as the buckets of water she'd carried at the camp.

As the plane had lumbered down the runway, engines rattling, Kia had held her hands over her tingling ears and closed her eyes. When she opened them, she was fascinated to see how far away the ground was, trees looking like new clumps of cabbage, roads no wider than the width of her pinky finger. She thought about the bombs dropped near her village and supposed that from up here pilots had no way of knowing where the bombs landed or how many people, good or bad, they killed.

On the long plane ride to America, Kia thought about what her mother had said. Somewhere over the ocean Kia tucked the cloth packet from her mother safely inside her coat and fell asleep dreaming of this new home called Minnesota, where she had been told the water turned to ice during the long, white winters.

9

Thek, a young Hmong who had come to America two years before, came to their apartment every few days. On afternoons when the sky looked dirty and hard and Kia's teeth chattered like knobby tree branches clattering in the wind, he took them for walks in the neighborhood. As they walked, Kia studied the people they passed. She had never seen so many people with hair the color of wheat and skin nearly as pale as cauliflower. And it seemed, in this land of so much, there was no silence to be found. Each night Grandfather said his ears were tired of the new sounds. Even the air smelled noisy, full of unfamiliar smells drifting out of doorways and lingering in the cold.

There was so much to learn that Thek forgot to tell them some of the simple things. The first night, when it was time for bed, none of them knew how to turn off the lights that blazed in the ceilings, so they slept with the lights on. It was only when Grandfather accidentally brushed against the light switch the next day that they learned how to shut them off.

At the grocery store they were speechless at the sight of aisle after aisle of food all packaged and ready to take home. They walked numbly past vegetables and fruits piled next to each other; cans of things they could only guess at; bags of rice, husk already off, ready to cook; chickens that had been cleaned and cut up. So much food for so little work, thought Kia, in amazement. America really did have everything.

"Here in America nothing is as it was in Laos," Thek told Grandfather sympathetically.

"It would be best to learn English as soon as you can so things will not seem so strange."

In the evenings, Grandfather pulled a chair to the window and gazed at the buildings that shut out the sky. Kia guessed he was remembering how important it was in Laos to be able to see a mountain from each house. Here, all he could see were whizzing cars on the black asphalt. In Laos, before a house was built, a hole was dug, and as many grains of rice as there were family members were placed in the hole. If the spirits moved the grain during the night, it was believed that the location was unlucky and another site for the house had to be chosen. She wondered how Americans chose places to build their homes. Maybe, she thought, because Americans already had so much, it did not matter to them if their homes were blessed by the spirits or not.

Alone at night in her room Kia slipped the ring she had taken from Ia onto her finger, held it up to the ceiling light, and admired the bloodred stone. She took out the picture she had torn from the magazine of the child sitting on her father's lap reading a book and studied it until it blurred before her eyes. It made her heart sad to look at them, but she tried to focus on the ring on the girl's finger. She told herself she was in America now, where everybody owned pretty things.

One damp afternoon when Grandfather was resting, Kia carried a basket of clothes to be washed to the laundry room in the basement of the building. It was a dingy room with cracked, tan walls and brown linoleum that had buckled from too much spilled water. As she heaved the basket of laundry onto the scarred table, she heard a husky voice say, "Quite a load for someone your size."

"Not so heavy," said Kia shyly as she measured the soap into the washing machine. When she tried to push the coins into the slots of the machine they would not go in. Looking over her shoulder, the woman said, "Honey, you got nickels there. You need quarters."

Blushing, Kia began pulling the soiled clothes from the machine and piling them into the basket again. She had mistakenly saved nickels instead of quarters.

She turned to face a chunky woman with bushy gold hair and electric blue eyes fringed by purple eyelashes. The woman wore shorts and a stretchy top that squeezed her around the middle so tightly that she reminded Kia of a snake that had just swallowed a mouse.

"Here. Just leave them clothes there. I've got a cupful of quarters. You can borrow some. Come on with me." Cheeks burning, Kia followed the woman down the hall to a door marked 2B, where a loud, clear voice announced, "And now, Sam the Sensational will demonstrate incredible agility as he juggles not one, not two, not three, but FOUR bananas!"

Shaking her frizzy, golden head, the woman muttered, "Oh, that boy," and opened the door onto a sun-washed room filled with green plants that spilled off tables and windowsills and pots hanging from the ceiling.

"Welcome to the Jungle Room," she said, gesturing toward the sunny room.

The moment Kia walked into the room, her heart began to smile. The room reminded her of her green mountain village in Laos, and a crashing wave of homesickness almost made her dizzy. She did not even see the boy standing in a shaft of sunlight until he said, "Hi. You must have come to see the show."

As though he had just been waiting for her to come, the boy began tossing bananas into the air with amazing speed. Kia had never seen anyone juggle before, and her eyes grew round as the bananas arced around the boy so fast they were nothing but a blur. Only when the woman snatched them from the air, one by one, exclaiming, "Sam, we can only eat so much banana bread!" did Kia notice that his arms and legs were shorter than her own, yet his face looked much older than Xigi's. His body was short and thick, and when he walked his stumpy legs swung out stiffly without bending at the knee. As he walked toward her, a blur of gray swung down from the curtain rod and perched upon the boy's head. Fascinated, Kia saw it was a tiny monkey with soft, wispy fur, small enough to fit into both her hands. Soft brown eyes peered at her from under a round black hat that sat crookedly upon his small head. He wore a miniature lemon-yellow vest and short knee-length pants. Kia laughed delightedly as the monkey bounced on the boy's head. The boy held out a stubby-fingered hand to Kia.

"Hi, I'm Sam. This is my mother, Hank. Her real name is Henrietta, but she likes Hank better. And this little scamp is Tiki. How 'bout I show you some real juggling? Hank, hand me those china teacups, will you?" The boy grinned impishly at his mother.

"Sam, Sam, Sam, what am I going to do with you?" Hank said as she gave Kia a fistful of quarters. "Sam thinks he's one of the natural wonders of the world and wants everybody else to think so too. He makes me crazy." Kia didn't know what the woman was talking about. It must not have been bad, she thought, because the woman smiled warmly at her son.

Sam turned his attention back to Kia. "I haven't seen you around before. You must have just moved in, right?"

"Yes. We just come." Kia could not take her eyes off Tiki, who chattered nonstop and repeatedly bowed and tipped his little black hat at her. The only monkeys she had ever seen were those in the jungle. They had been much bigger, and if you weren't careful they would sneak down from the trees and run off with a bowl or a piece of clothing that was drying on a bush outside the hut. When she was little her mother used to tell her if she wandered too far from the hut, the monkeys would snatch her up and take her to live with them in the treetops.

Sam carefully lifted the little monkey down from the top of his head. Scratching him under his impossibly small chin, he said, "Looks like we've made a friend, huh, Tiki?" He looked hopefully at Kia. "Maybe you can stay awhile?"

Regretfully, Kia shook her head as she started toward the door. She clenched her hands as she desperately tried to remember the English words she wanted to say. "I wash." She looked at Hank. "Thank you. I give you money tomorrow."

"Don't worry about it. Pay me back when you can," Hank said. Kia was halfway down the hallway to the laundry room when she heard Sam yell, "Come back tomorrow, then. I'm going to

teach Tiki how to juggle and he loves an audi-
ence! He's a real show-off."

She didn't know what the boy had said, but
she smiled anyway. As Kia pushed the quarters
into the washing machine, she thought how her
father would have laughed to see a monkey who
was as playful as he himself had been as a child.

That afternoon Thek brought them a letter. About twice a month a camp worker sent a
letter written in English from Kia's mother and
mailed it to the church for them, because Kia's
mother and grandmother could not write. As
Thek translated the letter, Grandfather leaned
forward in his chair, hands clasped together tightly
in his lap. The letter said that Grandmother was
in the camp hospital with stomach pains that
would not go away. She would not eat or speak to
Kia's mother, but would only stare at her with
blank, glazed eyes.

"'The American doctors say they can find
nothing wrong with her and they can do nothing
for her.'" Thek read aloud the words that the
camp worker had written for Kia's mother.

"'I think she is afraid. It will be good when

109

we are all together again. Has the church said when that might be?'"

"Why don't the doctors help her, Grandfather?" Kia wanted to know. "Grandmother would not say she was sick if she was not. The American doctors have bags full of medicine."

The old man rubbed his lined forehead with his thin, callused hand. "Sometimes a bag full of medicine is not what's needed."

As the sun set that evening Grandfather shuffled into his room to petition the good spirits to make Grandmother well again. Kia knew he was worried that the spirits would not be of help because he was so far away. She watched as he covered his head with his rumpled red shaman's veil and placed small bells carefully on the ends of his fingers. Quietly, she went to sit by the living room window. The musky odor of burning incense from Grandfather's room drifted out and she heard the faint tinkle of his finger bells. Grandfather's raspy voice chanted the healing words that he hoped would find their way halfway across the world to his ailing wife in Thailand.

The monotonous hiss of the traffic on the

street below made Kia drowsy. Little bursts of heat lightning played across the deep blue of the sky like streaks of light tossed about by giants. Low, distant thunder rumbled, promising rain. Though she knew her thoughts should be with her sick grandmother, memories of the playful gray monkey in the round hat and yellow suit kept popping up. Tomorrow she would ask Thek to help her write a letter in English to her mother and grandmother and tell them about the monkey and how he reminded her of her father. Maybe that would make Grandmother smile and forget her stomach pains.

It was now the beginning of May. Early spring in Minnesota had been cold and raw. Even with the heavy clothes Thek had brought, the wind still tore through them like the knife Kia had used to cut the *tauj* on the mountain in Laos. They did not know how to adjust the radiators in their apartment and they were ashamed to ask Thek, so during the day the southern sun beat in unmercifully, and at night it was sometimes so cold they wore their coats to bed to stay warm.

Nearly every day, Kia coaxed Grandfather into going to the grocery store with her. Kia carefully watched shoppers thump melons, smell peppers, and pick through strawberries. Still unsure of what things cost and the value of the coins, when it came time to pay for her items, she just opened the little coin purse she carried and trusted the cashier to take the correct amount of money.

Xigi loved watching the television given to them by a member of St. Mary's parish. Kia was surprised she understood many words and phrases, even though she did not always understand their meaning. Thek told Grandfather, who tired of seeing Xigi sitting in front of it all day, that it would help them all to learn English faster. It still seemed strange to Kia to see Xigi without the pencil stuck behind his ear, but he seemed to have lost interest in drawing. The sketches he had done in Laos lay on top of his dresser, forgotten.

As in the refugee camp, Grandfather did not make an effort to learn English. He worked on his *pa ndaus* and helped Kia plan one of her own. She thought carefully for several days before she decided what she would like to embroider. Because she missed home desperately, she wanted to tell about her mother working in the garden, hoeing the vegetables, the speckled chicken clucking on her shoulder. She needed to tell about her cousin, Wa, and how she loved her. And, since she needed to keep the memory of her father strong in her heart, in the corner of the *pa ndau* she would stitch a smiling child tumbling headfirst out of a basket.

Kia's working on her *pa ndau* pleased Grandfather but made Kia ache with longing for what had been. Her stitches were uneven and ragged and she was not proud of them. Still, she worked on it every day and did her best even when Grandfather insisted her stitches were too long and made her rip them out and do them again.

Sometimes, on a warm, inviting day, Kia would sit on the front steps of the apartment building, knees tucked under her chin, back against the sun-soaked brick. Often kids would gather down the street, and she would listen to their high-pitched laughter and wonder if she would ever have the courage to join them. One afternoon as she was watching them hop on one foot, a woman dressed in a black skirt and red blouse with a scarf tied over her hair and large sunglasses stepped out of Kia's building. She glimpsed Kia in the corner and turned to see what she was watching. Seeing the children, she laughed and turned to Kia.

"I remember playing hopscotch when I was that age. Always lost because I couldn't balance on one leg worth a hoot." Kia recognized her as Hank, the mother of the boy with the monkey.

Not understanding what the lady meant by *hopscotch*, Kia simply smiled at her.

Tilting her head toward the kids, she said, "You should go play with them. I'm sure you'd be better at it than I was."

Thinking the woman was going to take her over to the kids, Kia sprang up, alarmed.

"Thank you. Grandfather call." She pulled the heavy door open and clambered up the stairs two at a time. From the window of her apartment, she watched the woman walk toward the bus stop.

Kia had never seen the spring miracle of new leaves appearing on winter trees because it was always summer in Laos. She marveled that in such a short time, trees and bushes that had been brown as duck feathers turned a soft yellow-green. The air, unlike the humid, heavy air of Laos, was sweet and clean, making her want to take long, deep breaths.

It was a late May day, fragrant with the scent of the purple flowers that grew on the side of their apartment building, when Thek stopped to show them where their garden would be. He told them he had arranged for them to receive a permit to sell at the farmers' market in St. Paul. When Thek visited, he always spoke in English so they would learn the language faster. Grand-father scowled when he insisted upon this, but Kia and Xigi eagerly listened.

They were delighted to find out that the church owned the land across the street and was going to let them plant there. Grandfather was amazed that there was so much land just for them. Thek told them the church had recently purchased the three acres from the city and was planning on building a new school there. But since that was a few years off, Kia and her family and other Hmong immigrants, when they arrived, could grow vegetables to sell at the market to help earn money.

Together, she and Grandfather unfolded the packet of seeds Kia's mother had given her the day they left the refugee camp. They sorted through and separated the various seeds, some with little particles of black earth clinging to them. Kia held the seeds to her nose and smelled them. They smelled like home, and she felt her throat tighten with longing to see her mother and grandmother again. When Thek had learned of the mistake that left them behind, he announced he was going to Thailand soon to assist in refugee camps and would try to contact them. He said the members of the church were holding raffles and bake sales to raise the additional money needed to bring them to Minnesota, and as soon as enough had been raised, they would send for them. None of them knew what raffles and bake sales were, but Grandfather said if people they didn't even know were working so hard to help them, it was only right that they work hard to help themselves.

Grandfather and Kia walked to the corner of the busy street, waiting for the green light that meant they could walk, a frown pulling the corners of Grandfather's mouth down. Grandfather had asked Xigi to help them, but Xigi sullenly replied there was not enough for three people to do and remained inside watching the television, his foot restlessly tapping the floor.

Once Grandfather began poking the holes in which Kia dropped the seeds, his face softened. They worked until the final seed was in the ground, both thinking back to happier days when planting meant togetherness with their friends and relatives.

When they were finished, Grandfather was tired and crossed the street to go upstairs. Kia said she would soon follow, but wanted to be sure she had covered every seed.

Kneeling in the dirt of her newly planted garden, her green mountaintop village in Laos seemed very far away. Her chest tight with loneliness, Kia whispered, "Grow, little seeds, grow!"

As she crossed the busy street to the apartment building, she did not look at the two girls who stared at her and whispered behind their cupped hands. She pretended not to hear their stifled giggles and exaggerated laughter. Instead, she thought about later that night when she and Grandfather would return to the garden to ask the spirits of the field to protect their vegetables. For Kia knew that without the special blessing of the spirits their precious seeds would wither and die and they would not have beautiful vegetables to sell at the market and they would not be able to help earn the money to send for her mother and grandmother.

Kia wondered if she would ever be as wise as Grandfather. As they continued walking up and down the rows of green vegetables, Kia remembered when they had searched for herbs together on the village mountaintop. She had loved those early mornings with the sun dancing through the leaves because Grandfather always taught her something new and never minded how many questions she asked. He would show her cilantro, mint, fingerplant, and wild soybeans and explain how they were used to treat fevers. Those bright mornings had made her feel proud of her grandfather and all the good he did for the villagers. She came to understand how important and needed her grandfather was to the village.

But since coming to Minnesota, Grandfather had become more and more quiet. Men did not come to visit with him anymore to ask his advice, and there were no elders with whom he could share stories. There were times when Kia studied his thin, bowed body and felt there was nobody inside it. Here in America, Grandfather spoke only to Kia and Xigi, always using the old language, but that was not very often anymore. Sometimes Grandfather would talk with old Cha Lee, who was from Laos, too. During the war, Cha Lee had lost an eye and was nearly blind. He liked sitting in front of the grocery store in a pool of sunshine, listening to the babble of voices around him.

"Cha Lee worries that you are not strong enough to haul vegetables all summer. But strength is more than size and muscles. Real strength lies hidden deep inside."

"Like treasure, Grandfather?" asked Kia.

The old man tapped a bony hand upon his chest and smiled. "Like the most valuable treasure, Little Cricket."

Nearly every day Kia thought about Grandfather and his life in America. It seemed to Kia that the proud, lively man he had been in Laos was fading, like a bright cloth bleached by the sun, and she didn't know what to do about it. Her mother had said Grandfather's world was in Laos, and Kia wondered if he would, like the magazine picture, start blurring around the edges if she looked at him long enough, until he completely faded away, only to reappear in their village in Laos that he missed so much.

Once a week Mr. Davis from St. Mary's Church and his son Greg would come to visit and see how they were getting along. Thek had left for Thailand and had told them Mr. Davis would be their contact person until he returned in a few weeks.

Mr. Davis had big teeth that hung over his lower lip and tiny ears that hugged his head so tightly that from the front, he looked like he had no ears at all. Greg was just the opposite of his father. He had very small teeth with wide spaces in between and ears so large that when he stood in front of the window the sunlight glowed pink right through them like a rosy halo.

"Well, Mr. Vang, how are things going? We understand how difficult it must be to come to a new country and all, but you really need to attend these get-togethers we have at the church every Sunday night, you know. You'll meet lots of new people like yourself who are trying to get settled." Mr. Davis smiled so wide, Kia thought his cheeks would crack. "In order to be successful, you'll need to learn the lingo here, so to speak." Kia did not know what lingo was, but it must be something funny, because Mr. Davis laughed so that even the teeth farthest back in his mouth showed. Kia looked at Grandfather. She knew he did not understand a word of what Mr. Davis was saying, but he nodded his head slightly as though agreeing with him.

"Now, for this young man"—Mr. Davis motioned toward Xigi—"we think it would be helpful for him to jump right in, so to speak, and help with chores around the school and church. Oh, nothing too difficult, just things like cleaning, gathering trash, lawn mowing. Things like that. He'll be with others his own age who can show him how things are done here. The kids we hire pretty much run things for us in the summer when school is out. Greg here would be real happy to show you around. They're a good bunch of kids." Kia could see by the expression on Xigi's face that he was eager to get out on his own. Greg bobbed his head, like a chicken scratching for seed.

Despite Mr. Davis's invitations, Grandfather refused to go to the meetings at church. Instead he would sit in his chair at home and finger the *pa ndau*s he had brought with him from Thailand as if they told stories he never tired of hearing.

Twice the Davis family picked up Kia and took her with them. Mrs. Davis was a thin, pleasant woman with brown hair that kept falling across her forehead and into her eyes. Whenever she asked Kia a question, she answered it herself before Kia had a chance to reply.

"My, hasn't the weather been warm? But then, I suppose you are used to warm weather, aren't you? What a silly question, of course you are." Or, "I'll bet you're eager for school to start. I know I would be."

The meetings were held in the basement of the church, in the cafeteria where it was cool because of the big trees that made dancing shadows on the pale yellow walls. Kia and three other small Hmong children and their parents sat on high-backed wooden chairs and listened as a woman explained that only a handful of Hmong now lived in St. Paul, but they expected others to join them in the near future.

"We, that is the church, will help pay your apartment rent, gas, and electricity, as well as food and clothing, until you can find jobs to support yourselves." Kia tried to remember to tell this to Grandfather. She knew this would be important to him, because he believed people should help themselves. "That is why it is so important you all attend the English classes we have set up for you. If you can't speak English, life will be difficult and no one will hire you."

Kia felt her face get hot. She was sure the woman was talking about Grandfather. For the rest of the meeting Kia sat looking at her hands twisting in her lap.

One Sunday night, a couple of weeks after Xigi had started helping Greg and the other boys with the chores at school, he did not come home to eat dinner. Kia remembered how Xigi would often go off by himself back in Laos when there was work to be done. That night when Grandfather asked him where he had been, Xigi shrugged his shoulders and said he had met some new friends and he had lost track of time.

"Perhaps you would like to invite your friends here," said Grandfather. "I would like to meet some of your American friends."

Xigi had not even looked at Grandfather. "Yeah. Maybe."

Sometimes, on soft summer nights that buzzed with mosquitoes and traffic, Kia, hoping to make Grandfather talk, would ask, "Grandfather, is this the way you thought America would be?" or "Are you glad we have come to America, Grandfather?" And more often than not,

Grandfather would say, "We are here. We must be grateful." Then, he would run his bony hand down Kia's black hair and say in a teasing voice, "Your mother will not believe how you have grown." And because Kia knew she had not grown at all, she wondered if Grandfather was also teasing about being grateful to be here in America. Maybe he wished they were back in Laos, where Xigi would not miss dinner, and Grandfather and the other old men of the village could sit together in the cool of the long evenings and remember what it was like to be young.

Most of Kia's days were spent helping Grandfather tend the garden. Xigi was now rarely home for dinner and many times did not return until late at night. Kia would lie awake, waiting to hear the apartment door creak, and she wondered if Grandfather lay awake too. The next day Xigi would sleep until the hot noonday sun heated up the little third-story apartment to the temperature of the oven in their kitchen.

"We have to get a fan or something," Xigi would complain in English when he awoke.

"You know Grandfather does not

understand English," Kia scolded. "Why can't you speak so he knows what you are saying?"

"Why can't he learn English like everybody else?" was Xigi's retort. "He is just being stubborn."

In her heart Kia knew it was true. Several times she had tried to interest Grandfather in television shows other than the cartoons Xigi normally watched. Mr. Davis was becoming more insistent about Grandfather's attending the meetings at church, but each time the Davises stopped to pick them up, Grandfather would ask Kia to tell them he was not feeling well. So, Kia went to the meetings and sat through discussions she didn't understand about money and employment.

Usually, Kia went to the grocery store by herself. When Grandfather went with her, she would ask if he could read the aisle signs, but he would only shake his head impatiently, wispy beard wagging, and sharply ask Kia how much the tomatoes or rice were and caution her to count her change carefully.

At the store, Kia had trouble counting

money. It was one-eyed Cha Lee who spent some time helping Kia learn pennies from dimes and nickels from quarters. Although Cha Lee could barely see, he needed only to rub his rough fingers over any coin to tell what it was. He had a mouthful of blackened stumps where teeth used to be, and Kia wondered how he could chew. Cha Lee's shirt pockets bulged with the lemon drops he bestowed like gold upon the children who hovered around him. They loved him and told him riddles and jokes that he repeated to anyone who would listen.

On the days Grandfather went to the store with her, he and Cha Lee would often sit and talk while Kia did the shopping. Kia noticed that on those days Grandfather's voice became strong and interested again. She would remember the old days when people would walk many miles to get medicine for a sick baby or to ask Grandfather when would be a good time to build a new hut. Then she would remember what her mother told her back at the refugee camp and how American doctors there did not respect Grandfather's ways.

One humid, overcast morning when she and Grandfather were visiting with Cha Lee outside the store, Kia heard a woman scold her small son, who had cautiously joined the circle of children around Cha Lee hoping for a lemon drop.

"Patrick! Get away from them!" she barked at the child. She turned and remarked loudly to her friend, "These people shouldn't be allowed to hang around the doorway like this. Where are they all coming from, anyway?" The woman scowled at Kia and yanked the boy so hard by the arm that he stumbled to his knees. He started to cry. The woman swiped impatiently at the gravel that was stuck to his skinned knees and hushed him by saying, "See? Maybe next time you'll listen to me when I tell you to stay away from them." Numbly, Kia realized the woman was talking about them.

The boy, who only moments ago had eagerly placed his open hand on Cha Lee's knee hoping for a candy, turned and stuck his tongue out. Grandfather, Kia realized sadly, did not need to take English lessons to understand what the boy meant by sticking out his tongue at them.

The children that had been circling Cha Lee melted away and Cha Lee put the cellophane package of lemon drops back in his shirt pocket.

Xigi was home for dinner that night. Kia saw Xigi scornfully watching Grandfather as he stitched a *pa ndau*, sitting by the window to catch the last of the sun's rays.

"Women's work," Xigi said under his breath to Kia. But Kia liked to watch Grandfather's nimble brown fingers arrange the bright, intricate patterns and designs on squares of fabric. She knew each design told something about her heritage. The snails Grandfather carefully stitched onto the cloth were a symbol of family growth and togetherness, and the coil of the snails' shells symbolized all the generations before them. Along the edges of each square, he embroidered a border of triangles to keep evil spirits away from those who would buy the *pa ndau*. The eight-pointed star meant good luck, and the dragon's hard, bright scales protected the owner from sickness and death.

No matter how hard she tried, she could not embroider as well as Grandfather. And she did not care what Xigi said about embroidering, because when Grandfather sewed, the tired lines in his face smoothed out. She hoped, someday, Grandfather would be happy again as he used to be in Laos before their world was turned upside down. Before the war, before her father died, before the refugee camp, before coming to America.

It was when Kia worked in the garden that she thought most about her father. She worried that his spirit was restless and unhappy because he had been killed in the war, far from home and those he loved. Grandfather had told her that her father's souls would always live within her, and that she must never do anything to make him ashamed of her. He had explained that each person had three souls. When a person dies, the first soul stays with the body. The second soul wanders and goes to live with the dead person's descendants. The third soul goes back to the spirit world to be reborn and can be reincarnated as an animal or thing, depending on the person's past actions and luck. Kia knew her father had been a good man and had always tried to do what was right. She was sure he would return as something beautiful.

Sometimes when she was alone, Kia would whisper out loud to her father's souls and ask them to help make Grandfather happy again.

10

"Grandfather, how will we get the vegetables to market?" asked Kia one late July morning as they weeded the garden. With a mixture of excitement and apprehension Kia saw that soon many vegetables would be ready to pick. The hot, humid weather was making the weeds grow nearly as fast as the plants. Clouds of gnats hovered and droned around their heads. Although St. Mary's had given all of them some new clothing, Kia and Grandfather preferred to wear the long cotton pants and shirts they'd worn in Laos to help protect them from the thirsty mosquitoes, but they still had red welts on their necks and ankles that itched for days. Besides, Kia thought that if she wore the new soft-colored clothes it would make Grandfather feel farther away from home than ever.

The old man rested his callused hands upon his hoe and squinted down at his granddaughter. "One-eyed Cha Lee has a car, but his son needs it for work every day. Besides," said grandfather with a rare smile, "I am not sure Cha Lee should be driving. I do not think we would end up where we want to go." Kia also smiled as she thought of Cha Lee's poor eyesight.

"Cha Lee has a cousin," continued Grandfather, wiping the drops of sweat that ran down his narrow face, "who also takes goods to market each day, but Cha Lee says Shong Lue is a difficult man. I will think of another way to carry the vegetables when we take the bus." Grandfather paused for a moment then said, "I did not think it would be such a distance to the market. It is much too far to walk. There is a lot of space in this country."

Kia yanked up a stubborn weed. "Maybe Mr. Davis would drive us. He said to let him know if we needed anything."

Looking off into the hazy distance, Grandfather replied, "He has done too much for us already."

"He just wants to help us, Grandfather."

"That is so, but it is not right to ask for help from others when we can help ourselves. Back in Laos we took care of ourselves, and we will take care of ourselves here."

"Will the bus take us right to the market, Grandfather?" Kia fanned herself with her straw hat.

"Yes. But Cha Lee says we will need to get there very early to get a good spot. We will also need a table on which to sell the vegetables. That is a great deal to carry each day."

"Maybe Xigi can help us." Kia held her breath as she waited for Grandfather's reply, for she knew how disappointed and angry he was with Xigi.

"Xigi is too much of an American now to help us." Grandfather spat out the words as though they were a mouthful of spoiled fruit. "He works for a few hours a day at the school, but where is he the rest of the time? When he is home he watches television all day. He is too busy learning how to do nothing from his new American friends who drift day to day without purpose in their lives. Those who do nothing find trouble."

Kia hoped Grandfather was wrong. Back home in Laos, Xigi had always been quiet and liked to disappear by himself. But his quietness was different here. His eyes rarely looked into hers, and when they did, they darted away. He never said anything about his friends or what they did. She knew Grandfather had seen Xigi studying the magazines he brought home, magazines about clothes and music, and people who were famous only because they were in movies, not because they had done great things. Each day it seemed Xigi grew more distant and reluctant to speak the old language or follow Hmong customs.

Kia knew Grandfather also disapproved of Xigi's watching so much television. Although there was much Grandfather didn't understand, he knew the advertisements encouraged people to buy things they didn't have, things they were told they needed. He cautioned Xigi and Kia, "People on television say that buying things will make our lives better. It is only people who can make their lives better, not things. Americans seem to think money and what it can buy will make them happy."

When he said that, Kia reluctantly thought about Ia's ring, but she told herself it wasn't the same thing at all. Hadn't her birth necklace been stolen from her, the only thing she had left to remind her of her father? Wasn't her father dead and her family separated? She determinedly kicked Grandfather's remark to the back of her mind and told herself she deserved the ring, since she had nothing else.

Xigi had nearly become a stranger. During the few daylight hours in which Xigi was home, he barely paid any attention to either Kia or Grandfather.

"So, you have no time for us anymore, now that you have come to America?" Grandfather asked him. "Is this how your new American friends treat their families?"

Without answering, Xigi would stalk out of the apartment. Kia would watch him from the window until he was out of sight, fists stuffed into his pockets.

Once, when Grandfather was resting, she had asked Xigi why he did not bring his friends home. He had laughed and said in a hard voice, "They would think I live with a crazy man, the way Grandfather wears those veils and bells and moans to his spirits."

Kia was confused. "But, Xigi, the spirits called him to be a shaman. It's the way it's always been."

"My friends say they don't believe things like that here," Xigi had replied, not looking at her. "I'm not so sure I believe, either."

Remembering the packet of seeds from her mother, Kia said quietly, "If the war had not come we would still be living in Laos. What would you have done then? Would you still say Grandfather's way would not be your way?"

Xigi shrugged. "What difference does it

make? We are here now. I will not be like Grandfather, who lives only in his memories."

"What about Father?" Kia demanded. "He followed the old ways, like Grandfather. Do you think coming to America means we change from what we are?"

Raising his voice, Xigi stood up. "None of that matters anymore, Kia. Father isn't here anymore. I can't be like you and Grandfather, doing things the old way, wishing our lives were the same as they had been in Laos, because nothing is the same. With Mother and Grandmother still in Thailand, we aren't even a family anymore." Kia had never seen Xigi act like this. He was so upset, his voice broke. "Everything has changed and I'm going to change with it."

After Xigi had left the apartment, Kia sat for a long time and thought about what Xigi had said. It was true. Their lives had changed. She remembered what her mother had said about Xigi, that he would live in the make-believe world inside his head, if he could. Maybe that's what he was doing now, Kia thought, choosing to ignore his old life to get away from all the bad things that had happened. She didn't know how they could get far enough away from the war and the death of their father so that it didn't hurt anymore. Grandfather clung to the old ways, while Xigi wanted to forget them. Maybe, she decided, everybody had to make his own journey through the sadness. She wished they all could make the journey together.

Afternoons when Grandfather released her from struggling with her *pa ndau*, Kia went down to Sam's apartment. The little monkey was now used to Kia and would perch on her head and chatter loudly until Sam finally told him to hush or he would put him in his cage. Sam's mother, Hank, worked evenings as a waitress at a fancy restaurant and would often bring home food left over at the end of the night. Never tiring, always quick with a smile, Hank would set the table for lunch with her best dishes and silverware and pretend Sam and Kia were wealthy customers. For the first time in her life Kia tasted prime rib and lobster with garlic butter and orange sherbet the color of a rising autumn moon. Because there were still many English words she didn't know, she sometimes made Sam and his mother laugh until tears of violet mascara ran down Hank's cheeks and Tiki screeched with delight.

"Would madam like cream with her coffee?" Hank would ask Kia, bending slightly at the waist.

When she received no reply, she would ask again, "Would madam like cream with her coffee?"

Finally, looking solemnly into Hank's bright blue eyes Kia would say quietly, "I am very sorry, but I am Kia, not madam."

Kia did not know what was so amusing, but waited patiently until Hank caught her breath, for then she would explain it to her. Most times, even after Hank's careful explanation, Kia would smile, not because she understood what was funny, but because these good neighbors made her happy with their joyous and quick laughter.

Their garden across the street flourished. Kia was proud of it and several times asked Sam to go with her to look at it.

"Come see onion and beans," Kia said

excitedly. "So big! Mother say seeds grow good here. She not believe it."

But Sam would not be coaxed outside his basement apartment. "It's too hot," he said, glancing at the wavy lines of heat dancing off the street.

"We go early morning before sun hot."

"Too many mosquitoes."

"Wear long shirt and I give you hat," Kia offered.

"Nah, really, I'm allergic to bugs."

Kia thought a minute. "We go at night when sun gone."

Sam snickered. "Then I wouldn't be able to see anything."

Exasperated, Kia finally asked, "You ever go outside?"

Petting Tiki under his tiny chin, Sam replied, in a voice so low Kia could hardly him, "Not unless I have to."

So instead, Kia would bring Hank a few early radishes or shallots warm from the earth and Sam would teach her to play checkers and dominoes. But like a troublesome toddler, Tiki was not happy unless all eyes were on him.

The monkey loved to show off in front of Kia. Sam spent hours teaching Tiki how to juggle four green grapes without dropping one. Until Kia came, that is. Then, when he had Kia's undivided attention, Tiki would toss the grapes high and casually tilt his nut-size head back . . . and *plop! plop! plop!* into his mouth they would go until his little hairy cheeks bulged. Sam would yell and scold, but Kia was enchanted.

"Naughty monkey!" Sam scolded. But he could not stay mad at the fluffy creature, who crept onto his shoulder, batted his lashes, then bared his sharp little yellow teeth at him in an endearing monkey grin.

"Awww! I think I'll trade you in for a dog," Sam threatened, scowling at his pet. But Kia knew Sam would never part with Tiki. They were too much alike. Sam liked to show off for Kia as much as Tiki did.

One hazy afternoon as Kia sat with Sam while her clothes dried in the laundry room and Hank was at the store, Sam said, "How would you like to see a truly amazing feat with a pair of truly amazing feet?" Kia didn't understand exactly what he was talking about, but she watched with eager interest as he stripped off his shoes and socks and balanced on his head and hands, feet waving in the air.

"Now, kindly place one of those cucumbers on each foot." Kia did as she was asked and laughed in amazement as Sam spiraled the cucumbers rapidly through the air off the balls of his feet. Not to be outdone, Tiki squealed and somersaulted and backflipped across the sunny room until he had disrupted Sam's rhythm and the cucumbers thumped to the floor.

Thoroughly annoyed, Sam would pretend to ignore the monkey until Tiki began flawlessly juggling several plucked grapes and Sam would announce in satisfaction, "See! I told you he could do it!"

In Sam's house Kia was content. She did not have to wonder about Xigi and what he was doing late at night. And she did not have to be sorry that Grandfather sat alone in the quiet apartment stitching his *pa ndaus*, maybe remembering the days when he was strong and young and important.

The hot days continued. Finally, one morning Grandfather announced that tomorrow they would go with one-eyed Cha Lee's cousin to see how an American market was run. "Then," said Grandfather, "we will know what to do."

Cha Lee said his cousin, whose name was Shong Lue, was a lazy man who did not care how much he sold. He spent his summer mornings at the market dozing under a dirty baseball cap behind piles of dirt-encrusted onions and zucchini, making only an occasional sale.

"He is good for nothing, that one," Cha Lee warned them. "His wife works six days a week cleaning rooms at the motel. And they have five children at home! Every day Shong Lue says he will go back to Laos to his old mother and father where things were better."

Grandfather narrowed his eyes. "He is not happy working in America?"

Shrugging, Cha Lee answered, "I am not sure Shong Lue has ever been happy working anywhere. In Laos, Shong Lue worked no harder than he does now. Because he was sickly as a child, his family felt sorry for him and took care of him. He never grew up to be a man. Here, he can blame no one but himself for what he does not have." With a small laugh and shake of his head Cha Lee added, "Many times I have heard him scold his poor wife for working only six days a week instead of seven."

That evening when Xigi left the apartment, Kia walked with him to the corner. The sidewalk still held the heat from the day and the soles of her feet burned through her sandals.

"In a few days we will take our vegetables to market. It would make Grandfather happy if you would help us."

Xigi kicked an empty pop can into the gutter. "I spent enough time selling vegetables in the camp. I won't do it here too. I have other things to do."

Anger, like a firecracker, burst inside of Kia. "Grandfather is right. You do think you are too good for us now. Are you also too good to help earn money to bring Grandmother and Mother to America? Do you know Grandmother is sick? Do you even care? Sometimes, Xigi, I wish you had stayed back in the camp if this is how you are going to act! You are selfish and think only of yourself!" Hot tears filled her eyes, but Kia was determined they would not spill down her cheeks. She spun away from Xigi back toward the apartment building and sat on the outside steps until her breathing had slowed and her hands had stopped shaking. She would not upset Grandfather even more with her tears.

We do not need Xigi, she thought. We don't need anyone. Grandfather and I can do it on our own.

In her room that evening she took the red ring from her drawer and put it on her finger. She unfolded the picture of the girl sitting on her father's lap. As she did so, she thought about Ia and where she might have gotten the ring. Maybe she had bought it at the market in Laos from the men who traveled throughout the mountain villages selling goods. She might have found it lost and buried in the dust at the refugee camp. Or, she realized with a jolt, it could have been a gift from her father or someone she loved very much.

For the first time Kia understood that Ia

was not the only one who had lost something. When she took Ia's ring Kia had left behind her own self-respect. She thought about the driver of the car that took them to the camp, how he had grudgingly taken their birth necklaces and how angry she had been. The necklaces meant nothing to him except how much money he could get when he sold them. But for the Vangs, the necklaces had helped buy their freedom.

She forced herself to think about why she had taken Ia's ring. It wasn't just that she had wanted a pretty ring. Somehow she had hoped having the ring would help her forget her sadness. She thought about Xigi and supposed that he, too, was trying as best he could to find a way out from under the crush of sorrow.

Kia slipped off the ring and put it back in the drawer. Grandfather was right. People were far more valuable than things. Things were only objects you could hold in your hand or look at, not something you could hold in your heart. Nothing she would ever have would make her as happy as having her family together again.

II

Five o'clock the next morning found Kia and Grandfather squeezing into the back of Shong Lue's rusty pickup. Xigi, an arm thrown over his eyes against the rising sun, did not even stir when they left. Stacked next to Kia and Grandfather on the floor of the truck bed were brown paper bags of unwashed new potatoes, radishes, onions, and leaf lettuce. An old table and a ragged lawn chair were wedged in a corner. The bags toppled over with each stop and start of the bouncing truck, and Kia was kept busy chasing the rolling vegetables.

"It is a disgrace to bring such vegetables to market," said Grandfather loudly over the sound of the roaring muffler. "No wonder no one buys them."

Kia looked at her dirty hands. She tried to wipe them on the outsides of the brown bags, but the bags had been used so many times they shredded under Kia's touch.

"When we take vegetables to market I will polish them until they shine like jewels," Kia promised Grandfather.

He looked at her small, eager face and said, "I am glad I have my Little Cricket to help me. Together we will have the best stand at the market."

At last the rickety truck lurched to a stop. Kia looked around in surprise. She had expected the market to be held out in the country, as in Laos, with people walking along dusty roads, talking and laughing as they shopped. This market was right in the middle of the city, and everybody was in a hurry. Tall office buildings hemmed in the two-block area, and people were elbow to elbow setting out their goods. A big yellow-striped canvas awning stretched over most of the area, sheltering it from the broiling sun. Under the canvas everything looked sunny and bright. A big wooden sign read: ST. PAUL FARMERS' MARKET.

"This is a strange marketplace, isn't it, Grandfather?" asked Kia nervously.

He reached for the handwoven straw hat that had been hanging down his back and placed it on his head. Rubbing a hand over his eyes, he replied, "Everything is strange in this country, Little Cricket."

Shong Lue had found a narrow vacant spot between a man in bib overalls selling pots of flowers and a couple with bushel baskets of cucumbers. No one said anything as Shong Lue backed his truck into the space, but everyone was watching. When the fender of the truck knocked over a big basket of cucumbers, the flower seller shook his head and pursed his lips and shook his head again as though thinking, *I knew that would happen.*

"Hey! Watch what you're doing!" the man shouted, as the woman scurried to collect the rolling cucumbers.

Shong Lue kept repeating one of the few English words he knew: "Sorry, sorry, sorry."

Kia quickly bent down to help pick up the cucumbers and wiped them on her shirt before placing them back in the basket.

"Oh, you don't have to do that," the woman said. "I have an old rag here to clean them up with." From a back pocket she pulled out a piece of faded red flannel and began sorting and wiping the cucumbers. Kia watched the woman's large, freckled hands run the cloth up, down, and around the vegetables. When Kia felt the woman's brown eyes on her, she smiled slightly and ran back to Grandfather, who was helping Shong Lue set up the table. The table tilted badly to one side, so Shong Lue placed a flat stone under the short leg. Grandfather frowned. Kia could almost hear Grandfather thinking, *If that were my table, I would fix it right.*

One-eyed Cha Lee had been right. Shong Lue did not care if he sold anything. He carelessly dumped the vegetables in one big pile on the dented, slanting table, not bothering to separate them. He then planted his frayed lawn chair behind the table, folded his arms and closed his eyes, baseball hat pulled down to the bridge of his nose. Kia and Grandfather looked at one another, then back at the lightly snoring Shong Lue. At last, Grandfather turned away with a scornful "Bah!"

Across the street Kia could see a small park with neat cobbled pathways winding under huge, leafy trees. From a fountain in the middle, narrow ribbons of water snaked through the grassy area. As early as it was, there were half a dozen people walking their dogs. The park looked shady and cool, and Kia wished they had remembered to bring bottles of water.

The farmers' market was open from 6 A.M. until noon, and by 6:30 business was brisk. The aisles of neat, brightly organized fruits and vegetables reminded Kia of her grandfather's *pa ndaus*.

Kia folded and stacked Shong Lue's grimy brown paper bags on the ground for Grandfather to sit on while she wandered a few stalls away to see what others had to sell.

Now, there is a place where I would buy my vegetables, thought Kia as she passed two girls about Xigi's age putting fresh beans, potatoes, and onions into variously sized green plastic containers. The small ones sold for 50 cents; the middle-size ones were marked 75 cents, and the biggest containers were labeled $1.00. The baskets were filled with shiny vegetables, all the same size and length. Kia lifted one of the large ones to see how many onions were in it. One of the girls who had a rosy, sunburned nose and wore her hair in a long, blond braid down her back said in a friendly tone, "Do you want to buy that? It's only one dollar."

Looking up guiltily into eyes green as the sea, Kia quickly put down the basket. "N-no, just looking."

The girl smiled broadly. "They're the best vegetables at the market. And the best priced, too."

It was Kia's turn to smile. She could see the girl was as proud of her vegetables as Kia was of her own. I will have to clean and shine ours extra special to look as good as these, she thought. For the rest of the morning, while Shong Lue dozed, she and Grandfather quietly studied the American way of buying and selling vegetables, fruits, and flowers. Kia decided things were not so different here from in Laos. People still wanted good vegetables for a good price.

"But," said Grandfather, frowning, "here in America people have so much from which to choose. That is why lazy ones like Shong Lue are a disgrace."

At noon, everybody packed up their goods until the following day. Shong Lue had sold only a handful of radishes. With a deep sigh and mournful shake of his head, Shong Lue bagged his vegetables, dropping them carelessly upon one another into the limp brown bags.

"You see," he told Grandfather. "A man works hard for nothing. This very night I am going to make plans to go back to the old country. At least there a man could afford to live."

Grandfather did not reply. He, like Kia,

had walked around the market and had seen many things, but they had not seen anyone as lazy as Shong Lue.

Grandfather said no more about the way in which Shong Lue ran his stand at the market, but when Shong Lue said he would pick them up tomorrow if they wanted a ride, Grandfather quickly replied, "Thank you, we will manage on our own."

Shong Lue barely stopped the truck at the curb long enough for them to climb down from the bed of the truck before he disappeared in a fog of exhaust fumes. Bags of unsold vegetables tipped and rolled from side to side. They will be all bruised tomorrow, thought Kia.

"How will we get to the market tomorrow?" asked Kia later when she and Grandfather were picking the first of their vegetables just before the sun went down. A line of dark clouds was moving toward them and heavy rain was forecast during the evening hours. Kia had again asked Xigi if he would help harvest the vegetables before the rain, but he said he had things to do.

"We will take the early bus. Cha Lee says

the early ones are not so crowded. He told me where we get on and off." He showed Kia a rumpled piece of paper with some numbers and streets written on it.

"But, Grandfather, how are we going to carry so many things?"

Smiling, Grandfather said, "When Shong Lue first said he did not have room for us I sewed deep pockets in our long coats to hold many vegetables. We will look like pack mules, but we do not care."

For two hours they picked only the choicest vegetables and hauled them upstairs in baskets slung across their backs. They washed and sorted until their fingers were wrinkled and sore. They did not have little green baskets in which to display the produce, so they used brown lunch bags folded down at the top. With a black crayon Kia carefully wrote a price on each bag.

When Grandfather showed her the coats he had made she exclaimed, "Oh, Grandfather! They are perfect!" Kia put hers on and discovered it had two sets of long pockets that ran all the way from shoulder to hem around the entire coat. To prevent the vegetables from getting bruised they would pack the heaviest on the bottom, then layer crushed newspaper and place it between the more delicate vegetables on top.

Kia thought the coat was splendid and ran downstairs to show it to Hank and Sam.

"I've never seen anything like it," Hank exclaimed as Kia twirled around. "But remember not to sit down on the bus or you'll be selling vegetable soup!" They all laughed and Tiki screeched and grinned as though he knew what they were saying.

"I have a little something for you to take with you to the market," said Hank. She opened a closet door and from a shelf took down a snowy-white, square cloth. "At the restaurant, somebody burned a hole in this tablecloth, so they can't use it anymore. They were going to cut it up and use it for rags. Can you imagine such a thing? It's still perfectly good. If you set something over that little hole nobody will ever see it." With shining eyes, Hank held the linen tablecloth out to Kia. "Nothing but the best for the best vegetables at the market."

It was several moments before Kia took it. She fingered the soft white cloth, holding it at arm's length. In the center of the cloth, done in white silk just a shade darker than the linen, was a pair of birds perched on the bough of a tree.

"I . . . I not have this," Kia finally stammered. "I have nothing for you."

"But I don't want anything," Hank insisted. "I brought it home for you. The only thing I want is for you to like it." Hank looked closely at Kia through her purple lashes. "You do like it, don't you?"

Slowly Kia hugged the cloth to her chest. "It is beautiful. Thank you."

"Hey," Hank laughed. "It's only a tablecloth, not a mink coat."

"And, last but not least . . ." From behind his back, Sam whisked out a glass jar filled with dirt and a plant with large heart-shaped leaves, just like the ones hanging from the baskets by the window. "It's a philodendron," Sam told her. "Just put it near a window and watch it grow. Pretty soon it will be as big as those," said Sam, pointing to the ones by the window. "It's a tough little plant. But you need to add more dirt, 'cause that's all we had."

Kia looked around the green, sun-splotched room, then at Sam and Hank. "You good friends," she said in a husky voice.

"Yeah, yeah, yeah," said Hank, whose cheeks were pinker than usual. "Now. Just a final brush-up." Hank reached into her tight jeans pocket and brought up a handful of change. "Let's say I want to buy a bag of vegetables for seventy-five cents and I give you one dollar. How much change do you give me back?"

Ever since Kia had made the mistake of trying to put nickels instead of quarters into the washing machine Hank had teased her. "If old man Slater had walked in the laundry room instead of me, he'd have thought you were trying to cheat him and would have called the cops," she told Kia. Mr. Slater, a thin, balding man with squinty pig eyes, was the building manager. He talked so fast in a high squeaky voice, Kia could hardly understand him.

Confidently, Kia picked up a quarter and handed it to Hank.

"Good. Now, what if I give you this much money for two small bags?"

For half an hour Hank quizzed Kia until she was sure Kia could make correct change for every money combination she could think of.

"One-eyed Cha Lee taught you good," she told Kia. "Just remember to smile. People like to buy from people who smile." Hank faked a broad smile. Between stretched coral-tinted lips she said, "See? Isn't this better? Wouldn't you buy all your vegetables from someone who looked happy like this?"

Kia laughed and promised to smile. As she was leaving to go upstairs, Tiki decided to play hide-and-seek in her many coat pockets. He tickled Kia as he scrambled from front to back, in and out, his fluffy gray head popping up and down like a dandelion gone to seed. When Sam lifted him out, Tiki scolded him loudly and bared his sharp little teeth.

"Look here, you naughty little fuzzhead, you'd better look out or I'll trade you in for a poodle," threatened Sam, holding the little creature between his stubby hands. Looking full into

Sam's eyes, Tiki blinked and grinned from ear to ear.

Hank nudged Kia. "What'd I tell you? You can get away with anything if you smile nice."

That night, Kia showed Grandfather the tablecloth and the plant.

"Wasn't that nice of them, Grandfather? I think they will bring us good luck at the market, don't you?"

Putting his stitching aside, Grandfather examined the silk birds on the tablecloth. "They are very nice. But why would they give them to us when we have done nothing for them?"

Kia folded the tablecloth and put the plant on the windowsill. "The restaurant where Hank works was going to throw it out. She thought it would look nice on our table at the market." She studied her grandfather for a moment. "I think you would like Hank and Sam, Grandfather," said Kia quietly. "They are good people. Hank works very hard."

"Hmmm," murmured Grandfather. Kia looked at Grandfather's thin, tight, turned-downed lips and wondered why he showed no interest in meeting her friends. He did not mind if she visited them, but he never suggested she bring them to meet him. He smiled at stories of Tiki's antics and would remark, "He sounds like quite a character, this monkey," but that was all.

She sat down on the floor next to her Grandfather. "They are not like Xigi's friends, who think only about what they see in magazines, Grandfather. Hank and Sam don't think money is more important than people. They like me, Grandfather, and they would like you, too."

Still the old man did not answer. He simply put his *pa ndau* down and went into the kitchen to prepare supper.

After doing the dishes, Kia went outside to get more dirt from the garden for the philodendron. Big raindrops were polka-dotting the dusty ground, making juicy, plopping noises when they landed. The ground was still so hot, the drops disappeared in the dirt as soon as they landed. Using a spoon, she packed fresh dirt into the glass jar and went back upstairs. After adding a bit of water and gently patting the soil down on top, Kia looked carefully at her new plant. She could just barely see where the dirt Sam had put in ended, and where the garden dirt began. The wavy line ran all around the jar, like a decoration. Then, she thought she saw something move. She looked more closely and saw that she had scooped up an earthworm and that he was burrowing deeper into the soil. She laughed and said gaily, "Looks like you've got a new home, too, Mr. Worm."

She hurried into the living room to show Grandfather, but he was sound asleep in his chair by the window, the *pa ndau* that he had been working on lying colorful and quiet on his lap.

That night she dreamed Grandfather had found the ring folded up in the magazine picture in her dresser drawer. He held it out to her.

"Where did you get this ring?" he asked.

Shame burned in her heart like an ember from yesterday's fire. With lowered eyes she replied, "From Ia at the refugee camp."

"She gave it to you?"

Kia shook her head. "No."

"How did you get it?"

"I took it."

He paused. "Why?"

She started to sob loudly, hands covering her face. "I don't know! I know it was wrong!"

Grandfather said nothing for a long while. When her crying quieted, she finally lifted her eyes to discover she could look right through him, as if he were made of smoke.

"I'm sorry, Grandfather, I'm so sorry!" she cried. She ran to put her arms around him, but he evaporated into the air, the red ring spinning on the floor where it had fallen.

She woke up when it was still dark outside with sweat running down her temples, tangled up in her sheets. The dream had seemed so real, she thought she heard the ring still spinning on the wooden floor; but she finally realized it was the silvery tinkle of Grandfather's finger bells as he again pleaded with the healing spirits to make Grandmother well.

12

Rain was still dripping off the trees when Kia and Grandfather started for the bus the next morning. It had rained hard in the hours after midnight. Kia could tell by Xigi's muddy, wet shoes that he had not come home until late again.

Though the rain had stopped, the day was humid and overcast. Kia was hot and sticky inside her long coat. Every so often a welcome gust of wet wind nudged her a little more quickly down the street.

It was two blocks to the bus stop. Grandfather and Kia rustled when they walked. Kia clutched the white tablecloth and the little green metal box of change, while Grandfather lugged a folding card table they had bought at the secondhand store and used as their kitchen table. In addition to the long coats that were packed with vegetables, Grandfather and Kia each carried a woven basket on their backs brimming with yet more vegetables. Kia remembered when they had used these same baskets in Laos to harvest crops from the fields. It had been a joyous and thankful time filled with laughter and celebration. Sometimes she couldn't remember what it was like to wake up and not have to struggle with foreign words tripping up her tongue. And there were days when she felt imprisoned in the few small rooms of the apartment compared to the vast greenery of Laos.

At the bus stop Kia perched on one leg and absentmindedly rubbed the other behind it. A woman also waiting for the bus lifted her eyebrows at them and moved several feet away. The woman reeked of sweet perfume and wore very high heels with narrow pointed toes. They made Kia's feet ache to look at them. I would rather look like a pack mule than stink like that, thought Kia, wrinkling her nose.

"A little cricket like you had better keep both feet on the ground," said Grandfather as a great gust whipped the wet leaves on the trees, "or you'll be blown away. Then who will sell our vegetables?"

Grandfather was happy this morning, though his eyes were red and bags of wrinkled skin hung under his eyes. But Grandfather did not complain. Kia wondered if he was secretly looking forward to the excitement of the market. He did not appear to be worried that he could speak only a little English. After many unsuccessful attempts to coax Grandfather to attend the English classes at the church, Mr. Davis had decided it might be best to give Grandfather a few months to adjust to America before asking him to join them again. Mr. Davis, with Greg, still visited weekly, and Kia felt a little sorry for him because he tried so hard to be helpful. Kia had not told Mr. Davis about her and Grandfather going to the market.

In addition to the vegetables they had brought, Grandfather had completed five *pa ndau*s to sell. He had finished four in the refugee camp and one since coming to America, each different from the next. Embroidered on them were designs of roosters' combs and birds' wings and frogs' legs. Kia liked the dragon's-tail design, with its beautiful satin chain stitching done in bright reds and greens. It made her feel bold and strong.

Her favorite *pa ndau* was the one that showed men and women picking corn back in the green fields of Laos. Children watered the pigs, and butterflies flitted among the trees. Kia wondered if the man plowing the field behind the water buffalo was meant to be her father. Many times she had seen him do this, quietly coaxing the animal forward. She ran a finger over the fine stitching and forced herself to swallow the lump that grew in her throat and burned her eyes. She wanted to ask Grandfather about it, but she didn't want to make him unhappy this morning when he seemed to be looking forward to the day at the market.

The bus finally came and the woman in the high heels climbed quickly aboard. She sat behind the driver who watched suspiciously as Grandfather hauled the table up the bus steps. Very carefully Kia dropped the coins into the slot and followed Grandfather to the rear of the bus where he propped the table against some empty seats. Cha Lee was right. There were few people riding the bus at this early hour of the morning. A man in a business suit reading the newspaper did not even look up as they passed, and a tired-looking woman in a white uniform stared out the window. One time when the bus lurched to avoid a swerving car, Kia was nearly thrown onto the seat behind her, and she smiled as she thought about what Hank had said about having vegetable soup to sell at the market if she were not careful.

When they got off the bus, people at the market were hurriedly unloading trucks and unpacking boxes. Under the bright yellow canvas top, Kia breathed deeply the aroma of herbs and ripe vegetables. A great longing swept over her as she watched these bustling, unsmiling strangers. She wanted nothing more than to be in her mountain village in Laos, laughing and joking with her cousins as they pounded the rice, separating the outer shell from the white grain, as she had done for Aunt Zoua. What was she, Kia Vang, doing so far from home, so far from everything that she knew?

She stood still, lost in thought, until Grandfather said gently, "Come, Little Cricket. We must find a spot before there are none left." It was only with great effort that she forced herself to remember where she was and what she must do.

Late that night Kia lay listening to the ticktock of the alarm clock on her dresser. From the apartment below, a radio thumped its way through song after song. In her mind, Kia relived the whole horrible day, wondering where it had started to go so wrong.

They had set up their table between a heavy man with dark, curling hair on his arms selling early sweet corn and strawberries. On the other side was a family with a trunk full of rhubarb. The children were eating from a bag of powdered doughnuts that left gooey rings of white sugar around their lips.

Kia had proudly spread the white cloth on the old table, making sure the hole was covered, while Grandfather unloaded their baskets. Checking to be sure the vegetables had not bruised, they set out the small paper bags according to price and variety. She had placed Grandfather's *pa ndaus* at the very front of the table. Against the snowy white tablecloth the *pa ndaus* looked cheerful and friendly.

Just before the market opened, Kia quickly compared their table to others around them. From a distance she saw Shong Lue settled sleepily in his chair behind his lopsided table. Then she walked slowly past the stand she had admired that was run by the two girls. It is nice, thought Kia, but ours is better. The blonde with the long braid and green eyes looked up as Kia passed.

"Come to buy this time?" she asked pleasantly, tilting her head to the side as she looked at Kia.

Remembering Hank's advice, Kia gave the girl a shy smile. "No, we here to sell, too."

The girl's head snapped up and her eyes were wide. "You have a stand here at the market?" Her voice rose to an incredulous squeak.

"Yes."

"Where?"

Kia pointed across the aisle to Grandfather standing with his hands tucked into the wide sleeves of his shirt. His eyes were fastened on the ground in front of him. I must remind him to smile, too, thought Kia.

After a long pause the girl said, "Well, good luck." The friendly smile was gone, and even though her words were polite, Kia did not think she meant them. Kia hurried back to Grandfather.

"Our stand is the best," she whispered to him. She was about to tell him what Hank had said about smiling when she saw the two girls from the other stand slowly approaching their table. Kia smiled nervously as they fingered the tablecloth and studied grandfather's *pa ndau*s.

"What are these?" asked the blond girl picking up the red-and-green dragon's-tail *pa ndau*.

"They flower cloths," replied Kia. "Tell stories of Hmong."

The girl examined the *pa ndaus* with a puzzled expression. Kia tried to think how she could explain them better. She thought of the photo albums she had seen at Sam's. "They like pictures of family."

The blond girl dropped the flower cloth carelessly on the table. "I don't get it," she mumbled to her friend as they started walking back toward their own stand. "Do you?"

The girl's friend glanced back at Kia and said, "No, they're weird, if you ask me."

Kia had never heard the word *weird* before and had no idea what it meant, but from the girl's tone of voice she didn't think they liked the *pa ndaus*.

Forcing herself to smile, Kia straightened the flower cloths. Kia looked at Grandfather, standing so straight and proud beside their table. She thought of all the hours he had worked on them until his eyes were strained and red. She thought of her mother and grandmother back in Thailand waiting patiently behind the barbed-wire fence. She brushed a piece of dirt from one of the cloths, lifted her chin, and smiled a little brighter.

The morning passed more slowly than mud running uphill. Many people stopped to peek into the bags of vegetables and look at the embroidered cloths, but they all went away empty-handed. Kia kept smiling even when she heard one man mutter, "Well, they look clean enough, but you just never know. They're a different kind."

By noon the lovely white cloth was streaked with dirt from curious fingers, and the small metal green box had not been opened even once. Kia and Grandfather repacked their wilting vegetables and stood silently among the tired passengers during the long bus ride home.

That afternoon Grandfather was taken sick. His thin shoulders shook with chills and beads of sweat dotted his forehead. Except when he had returned from the war, Kia could not remember Grandfather having ever been sick.

"I am just tired," he told Kia, but when he

picked up his embroidery work, his hands trembled, and his normally beautiful stitches were loose and uneven. Finally, he put his work in the basket and went to his room to lie down. Kia waited until his breathing was deep and regular with sleep before she slipped out the door and across the road to the garden. She looked up and down the rows at the quickly ripening vegetables. She tried to admire the tall, healthy plants, but she was seized with a wild desire to yank them all up by the roots. Fists clenched, she sank to her knees in the moist dirt.

What is wrong, she kept asking herself, why did no one buy from us? There was no cleaner or bigger produce than theirs to be found in the entire market! She had smiled the whole morning until her cheeks ached. The tablecloth had been spotless, at least in the beginning. And she knew their vegetables were not priced too high, because she had compared them with others the day they had gone with Shong Lue. Other stands at the market had all seemed to be enjoying a brisk business except theirs. And maybe Shong Lue's, she admitted, but his produce was unwashed and

unsorted and he hid underneath that filthy baseball cap and never looked up. She could understand why no one wanted to buy from him.

From across the street Kia heard shrill
voices and looked over her shoulder to see the
girls from the next apartment building standing
toe to toe.

"If you don't do what I tell you, I won't
play with you! It's my chalk and you have to do
what I say!" one of the girls shouted. She stood
with her hands on her narrow hips and her head
lowered like a bull ready to charge. The other girl
threw up her arms and yelled, "Chalk? It's only a
stupid rock! I can get one anywhere!"

Kia studied the two girls. One wore a
light-blue short outfit the color of a robin's egg
with a matching hair ribbon holding her golden
hair away from her angry, flushed face. The
other girl had on a pale yellow dress with a big
sunflower painted on the front and wore her
curly, light brown hair in a fat ponytail. The
ponytail bounced up and down the girl's back
like a spring.

In the same way a dewdrop magnifies a

single blade of grass, Kia saw them clearly for the first time. She saw their pretty summer clothes and she remembered how they giggled and whispered whenever she passed them. She remembered the lady wearing too much perfume at the bus stop and how she had moved away from Grandfather and herself. She remembered the look in the blond girl's eyes at the market when she had told her she and Grandfather had come to set up a stand. She thought about the bus driver; how he had stared at them like he didn't want to let them ride his bus. Finally, she remembered the look of distaste on the man's face at the market when he had said, "They're a different kind."

Kia looked down at her shapeless, dark cotton pants and blue collarless shirt. There was dirt under her ragged nails from digging in the garden. The heels on her rope sandals were worn and badly frayed. Slowly, like something she did not want to do but couldn't help doing, she slid her hand down her straight black hair and knew she would never have a light-brown, curly, bouncy ponytail. Or golden hair that danced in the sunshine. Or green eyes the color of the sea.

Her mother had said she and Xigi would make a place for themselves in America, and she had tried hard to believe that. At school in the refugee camp the teachers had told them people from all over the world came to live in America. She wondered where they all were, and if they were as unhappy as she.

13

When Xigi came home late that afternoon
Grandfather was still resting in his room. Xigi's
hair had grown long and shaggy since coming to
America. In the refugee camp, boys had kept
their hair short to keep it clean and to stay cool.
Now it hung down over his ears in sharp spikes
and halfway into his eyes, so that he had to keep
brushing it off his broad forehead.

Each afternoon Xigi changed into a white
T-shirt and blue jeans before he left for the
evening. Once, when Kia had asked him why he

did this, he had mumbled something about all the guys wearing them.

"Where is Grandfather?" asked Xigi, looking around the room.

"Grandfather isn't well. He's resting." She took a deep breath. "Xigi, I need you to go to the market with me tomorrow morning since Grandfather is sick. I can't carry all the stuff myself."

Xigi shot a sharp, disgusted look toward Kia. "I told you, I am not going to sell vegetables. Besides, I can't. I'm busy." For a moment Kia thought Xigi was going to say more, but he wheeled away from her.

Clenching her hands, Kia spoke quietly so as not to disturb Grandfather. "Xigi, the more money we can help the church make, the quicker Mother and Grandmother will be able to come here, you know that. We need to be together again. Right now, selling our vegetables is the only thing we can do to help. And we have so many vegetables that are ripe. We can't let them rot, after all our work." Tears of tiredness and frustration filled Kia's eyes. Her throat swelled like grains of rice dropped in hot water and she could hardly swallow.

"How much did you sell today?" asked Xigi in an accusing voice.

Recalling the humiliating day, Kia whispered, "Nothing."

Xigi's black eyes widened. "Nothing? Not one thing?"

Kia shook her head, swallowing hard.

"So, what makes you think you will sell something tomorrow, or the next day, or the day after that?"

Looking him straight in the eye, Kia said quietly, "Because we have to."

"Well, you'll have to do it without me, that's all." He started toward the door as if he couldn't get away fast enough. With his hand on the doorknob, he stopped and added, without turning around, "Kia, I wish I could help you. But, I just can't, that's all." Then he spun on his heel, and the door slammed shut behind him.

The next morning Grandfather was no better. His eyes were sunken pits, and he still shivered with fever. A northwest wind had sprung up overnight and had dropped the temperature to a welcome 62 degrees. At least, Kia thought, the vegetables not yet picked will last a little longer in this cool weather.

Sometime during the long, wakeful night Kia had decided there was nothing to do except ask Shong Lue if he would take her with him to the market. She would offer to wash and sell his vegetables as well in return for the daily rides until Grandfather got his strength back. She was getting ready to go to the grocery store to see one-eyed Cha Lee to find out where Shong Lue lived when she heard Grandfather call weakly from his room.

As though he had read her thoughts, he said, "Do not worry. I will be up in a day or two." Through chattering teeth he said, "Little Cricket must not try to do everything by herself."

She tucked the worn blanket around Grandfather's thin shoulders. "I am not worried, Grandfather. But it would be a shame to let our vegetables go to waste. I am sure Shong Lue would be happy to take me with him. Then he will have someone to listen to his complaints." A slight smile lifted the corners of Grandfather's lips. He closed his eyes and Kia slipped out of the apartment and down the stairs.

In the hallway she met Hank lugging groceries. Kia took one of the bags from her and followed her down to her apartment. Tiki chittered with delight when he saw Kia and swung from the curtain rod to the couch and back again, tipping his little porkpie hat at her as if she were a great lady.

"That monkey doesn't know what to do with himself when Sam's sleeping. He's going to drive me crazy. Whew! I don't know why I packed these bags so heavy," Hank said, thumping her bag down on the kitchen counter. "If you hadn't come along, I would have dropped them both." She began putting the groceries away. "So, how'd it go at the market the other day? Did they clean you out?"

Kia scooped Tiki up and he scrambled to perch on the top of her head. "We are new. People not buy yet." She kept her eyes on Tiki so she would not have to look at Hank.

Hank narrowed her blue, violet-lashed eyes at her. "Didn't go so good, huh?"

Kia sighed. "Not so good. But," she added, "cloth beautiful. Everybody touch it. I go to market with Shong Lue till Grandfather better."

"Your grandfather is sick? What's wrong with him?"

"He say just tired."

"You let me know if he's not better in a day or two and I'll make him some chicken soup. That'll fix him right up."

When Kia didn't reply, Hank cupped Kia's chin in her hand and forced her to look at her. "Do you hear me?"

Kia nodded shyly as she watched Hank's strong, capable arms rearranging items in the cupboard, and wondered what Grandfather would think of this woman with her bush of frizzy golden hair and purple lashes. He would probably say Hank was just another strange thing in this country full of strange things.

As Kia was preparing to leave, Hank placed a rough-knuckled hand on her shoulder. "You know, Kia, sometimes you don't think things are ever going to work out. But they do. They always do. It just takes time." She made a wry face and gave a little snort. "I know what it's like to carry so much worry around you can hardly lift your head up. Here, sit down here with me for a minute." They sat next to each other on the couch while Tiki perched next to an open window. Whenever a breeze blew his fine, gray fur he tsk-tsked and scolded furiously, snatching his tiny hat off his head and slapping it on his miniature knee.

Hank did not face Kia but looked straight ahead. "They say time heals everything. Well, I don't know if it heals everything, but it does help a lot. When Sam was born, the doctors knew right off that he wasn't like other babies. 'Course, I thought they were crazy. What could possibly be wrong with my beautiful baby? Oh, they tried to be nice and told me he wasn't retarded or anything. They said he'd probably be real smart. He just wouldn't grow like other kids. Physically, he wouldn't be like them." Hank was silent for several minutes. Kia looked down at

Hank's large, strong hands, palms up, lying quietly in her lap. She thought they looked strangely helpless, like bloated fish stuck in the reeds of the Mekong River. She remembered gazing at her mother's hands as she slept, the morning after the soldiers had come to their village. Their hands, she thought, were as different from each other's as the women themselves.

"Well," Hank continued in a flat voice, "they were right and I was wrong. But don't think I ever admitted it. I just kept telling people, his dad was short when he was a boy, too. Just wait, I told them; one of these days, Sam will shoot right up and be the star of the basketball team." Hank gave a sad little laugh. "Nobody was going to tell me my kid wasn't perfect. I thought I could make him perfect by just pretending that he was. Except I couldn't. Pretty soon I stopped taking him places because people called him a munchkin and asked if he lived in the Land of Oz, and I couldn't stand that. By the time I realized that I couldn't make him perfect, Sam was so used to my making excuses for the way he looked he never even got a chance to like himself. He was convinced I didn't want him the way he was."

Running a hand through her wild hair, Hank, her blue eyes wide, turned to Kia. "But it was never true! I love him more than life itself. But it was a terrible thing I did, trying to pretend he was something he could never be. I know Sam would never admit it, but he's lonely, cooped up in this house all day. But I keep hoping. There isn't a morning that I don't wake up and pray that maybe today will be the day Sam will say he wants to go see a movie advertised on TV, or to the park, the zoo, or a baseball game. Just someplace." Sighing deeply, as if she was too tired to continue, Hank said, "But I guess he'll just have to decide for himself if he wants to spend the rest of his life in this little apartment. But it's no way to live, Kia, it's no way to live."

Kia did not know what to say. She couldn't understand everything Hank said, but she could understand that her heart was troubled. No grown-up had ever spoken this way to her. She could sense that just talking about it had brought Hank a kind of peace. The two of them just sat there, side by side and silent, until Tiki, screeching wildly, scampered from the window into the kitchen, returning with a huge cluster of green grapes. He scrambled to the top of the curtain rod and began pelting Kia and Hank with the grapes.

"You naughty little scamp!" laughed Hank, standing on the couch and snatching the grapes from the monkey's tiny hand. "I think you lie awake at night thinking of things you can do to cause trouble. Now, make yourself useful and go get Sam up before he sleeps the day away." At the mention of Sam's name, the monkey skittered down to Sam's closed bedroom door and began swinging from the doorknob.

"Don't forget what I said," Hank told Kia as she walked her to the door. "Just wait and see. Everything will be all right. And if you need that chicken soup, just holler."

When Kia reached the front door of the apartment building, she saw the two girls next door were playing jump rope on the front sidewalk. Before they could catch sight of her, Kia turned and slipped back down the hallway and left by the back door of the building.

Shong Lue happily agreed to take Kia to the market with him. She knew it was only because she offered to do his work for him that he wanted her along, but she didn't care. By evening Kia's fingers were stained and wrinkled from washing not only Shong Lue's vegetables, but also the newly ripened ones from their own garden. After this, she told herself angrily, I will not make bargains with lazy people like Shong Lue.

She had been afraid the soiled white tablecloth would not come clean after the first disastrous market day, but she scrubbed it by hand in the bathtub, and in the deepening twilight, it glowed soft as moonshine. She went in to show it to Grandfather, and he had nodded his approval.

The next morning Kia made many trips downstairs with bags of vegetables to load into Shong Lue's truck. When she had said good-bye to Grandfather he claimed to feel stronger, although his face was damp and waxy looking. Assuring him that she would be gone only until one o'clock, Kia placed a fresh glass of water on the floor by Grandfather's bed and waited outside on the curb for Shong Lue.

When they reached the market and Shong Lue had managed to park his truck without any problem, he was quite happy to let Kia set up the tables while he slouched in his chair and sipped coffee from a thermos. Even when there was work enough for two it did not bother him to just sit and watch. She tried hard not to dislike him, but each time she heard him noisily slurp his coffee, then suck his lips in satisfaction, Kia felt a surge of anger in her heart that nearly choked her.

"Your grandfather is fortunate to have a helper," Shong Lue commented when Kia had finished displaying the vegetables. "It is not good for a man to work too hard."

Knowing she should not talk back to her elders, but unable to stop herself, Kia replied firmly but quietly, "Grandfather believes everyone should do something worthwhile, no matter what it is."

Loudly sucking a sugar cube, Shong Lue replied, "Something, yes. But one must not work all the time."

"One must not be a burden, either." Kia knew she was saying more than she should and that Grandfather would not approve. But, how dare this lazy man whose wife and children supported him talk to her about work! With great effort she said no more but watched the steady trickle of shoppers. After a few minutes, her eyes slid over to Shong Lue and she saw he had already dozed off, slouched low in his chair, his breath making wet, wheezing sounds through his stained teeth. His greasy cap shielded his eyes and coffee stains dotted his shirt. It would have been best if he had stayed home, thought Kia disgustedly. But there was nothing to do but make the best of it. Taking a deep breath, Kia straightened her shoulders, relaxed her face into a little smile, and stood between the two tables.

Kia had stood there for what seemed a very long time numbly watching shoppers visit all the stands except hers when she heard a familiar voice cry, "Oh, there you are! I've been looking all over for you."

Separating herself from the sea of people was Hank in a flaming orange sundress, carrying a wide-brimmed straw hat that trailed a ribbon of the same color. She had done something to her hair so that it lay slick and golden against her head instead of frizzy and flyaway. On her feet were white, open-toed, high-heeled sandals that made her seem at least three inches taller. Over each shoulder she had slung two large mesh bags.

Grandly sweeping up to Kia's table she exclaimed, "Darling, I was so afraid you hadn't come today! And, you know what Chef Casini would do to me if I showed up at the restaurant without your fabulous tomatoes and onions! Why, I might as well lie down and die right here! He would simply never, ever forgive me, that's all." Hank's eyes swept over Kia's table.

"Now," gushed Hank, "I think you have everything I need. After all, a chef is only as good as his ingredients, you know." She gave Kia's brown cheek a pinch, then rattled around in a voluminous pocket for a crumpled piece of paper. From where Kia stood, she could see that it was totally blank.

Finger against her coral lips, Hank pretended to study the list. She appeared to be checking the items on the list against the items on Kia's table. Several shoppers at neighboring stands had stopped chatting and were gazing at Hank in fascination. Kia was frozen into complete and absolute silence.

"As usual," Hank announced loudly to Kia and everyone else at the market, "you have exactly what I need! Oh, I hope I won't clean you out, but Chef Casini would just skin me alive if I didn't get everything he needed. Let's see. If you would just hold this bag open, " she said to Kia, "I'll just start filling his order."

With brief glances at the paper in her hand, Hank dumped sack after sack of Kia's vegetables into her mesh bags. Every so often her violet-lashed eyes would twinkle into Kia's deep brown ones, and Kia would feel a great bubble of laughter fight its way from her stomach to her lips. Kia glanced at the shoppers, who were as mesmerized by Hank as she was.

Hank inspected several tomatoes. "These are even redder and juicier than the ones you had last week! Chef Casini will be ecstatic! How do you do it? Oh, well, never mind. I don't care how you do it, just so you do it. Now, according to my calculations, I owe you . . ." And Hank named what seemed an enormous sum to Kia, who looked at the scattered, empty bags on which she had so carefully written prices. Hank had bought half her produce. Looking like an exotic orange bird, Hank sashayed her way down the crowded aisles and toward the street with every eye following.

"See you in a few days and be sure to save the best for me!" she called over her shoulder to Kia. "Keep those scrumptious vegetables coming!" The crowd of shoppers parted as Hank tottered down the street on her high heels.

Kia looked down at the money Hank had given her. Knowing she would remember this moment for the rest of her life, she retrieved the little metal box from under the table. With a click of her thumb, the lid sprang open. One by one she smoothed out the rumpled bills and placed them inside. She closed the lid and felt very rich as she heard the coins slide from side to side as she placed the box back under the table. Just to be safe, she slid it out from under the table and put it on the ground beside her, firmly placing her foot on its lid.

Whispering and muttering to themselves, the crowd slowly went about its business. Every once in a while, someone would look back at the small girl with her foot on her money box. Across the aisle, Kia saw the girl with the long blond braid staring at her. Beside her sat an old woman with a humped back and a creased, puckered face, like an apple that had been dipped into a pot of boiling water. She was saying something to the girl while pointing toward Kia with her black cane. Kia could not hear what she was saying, but the blond girl with the sea-green eyes flashed Kia a tight smile. For the rest of the morning, a steady stream of customers kept Kia busy.

Shong Lue woke up with a startled snort and groggily asked if it was time to go home yet.

14

"So, who was this woman that bought all your vegetables?" Shong Lue demanded as his old truck sputtered its way home. He was angry that he had slept while this orange vision had bought up all of Kia's goods. "And why did she not want mine if she was buying for a big restaurant? Restaurants need lots of vegetables."

Kia was still dazed by the morning's event and did not know how to answer Shong Lue, because she herself did not know exactly what had happened or why. "I do not know why she did not buy yours, Shong Lue," she kept repeating until the truck lurched to a stop in front of her apartment building.

As she was collecting her baskets and struggling with the table, Shong Lue said sullenly, "I cannot give you a ride anymore. I am seeing about going back to the old country where a man can make a decent living to feed his family." His face was dark with anger, and he kept staring at her green metal money box as if he wanted to snatch it from her.

Glad that he could not read her thoughts, Kia stood and watched him jolt away from the curb, his truck belching a stinking cloud of smoke. She was glad the two girls next door were not outside. She had just pushed open the heavy outside door when Hank hollered from downstairs.

"Darling! Come down here and tell me all about your day!" Sam, Hank, and Tiki stood eagerly before her like children waiting for presents. Hank had taken off her orange dress and had squeezed herself back into a tube top and shorts. For a moment Kia wondered if she had dreamed the whole thing. But a glance at their kitchen table, heaped with her vegetables, made her realize it was not a dream. She began to giggle. Soon they were all three laughing uncontrollably, with Tiki grinning and screeching as he leaped from curtain rod to chair to couch. Hank insisted on playing out the entire scene for Sam, who laughed so hard he started to cough and choke.

"I would have given anything to have seen that," he said, holding his stomach. "I'll bet you were really something."

"As a matter of fact, I was," agreed Hank. "But then, I always did want to be on the stage." She hugged Kia close. "Anything for our little friend here. And, besides, I got the best deal in town."

Kia looked up into Hank's bright eyes. "This really all for chef?"

Hank raised her eyebrows and looked at Kia in mock surprise. "You bet it is! Chef Casini really is the cook at our restaurant and he'll go crazy when he sees all this! He hasn't had vegetables like these in his kitchen since I started working there. Oh, he always has fresh stuff, but nothing like this." A sneaky smile played on Hank's lips. "In fact, if I wasn't such an honest soul, I'd charge him double for what I paid for them plus a delivery fee." Hank glanced at her watch. "I'd better get a move on so I can get there before he does. And, Kia, if your grandfather isn't better by tomorrow, let me know." She winked at Kia and went to her room to change clothes.

Sam walked to the door with Kia. "I guess she was really something, huh?"

Kia smiled and nodded. "She act like tiger."

When Kia entered the apartment, Grandfather was sitting in the living room. His face had some color again, and Kia wondered if the letter he was holding was the reason. "Thek is back from Thailand and has brought another letter from the refugee camp. He says your grandmother is feeling better. Your mother is proud of the garden we grew," he added, "and cannot wait to see it." Kia smiled and wondered how many times Grandfather had repeated to himself all that Thek had read so that he would not forget a single word. Running a finger over the words he couldn't read, Grandfather continued, "Thek says that every day they ask the light-haired woman when they can come to us. The woman said it should be within a few months."

For the first time in a long while Kia felt hope rise in her chest like a soap bubble floating on a breeze. Soon they would be a family again.

When Grandfather had carefully folded the letter and put it back in its envelope, Kia gleefully told him what had happened at the market. The old man watched Kia intently as she described how Hank had made sure that nearly every shopper had heard her exclaim over Kia's wonderful vegetables.

"You should have seen them, Grandfather! When Hank left, they nearly ran over each other to buy the few bags of vegetables I had left. People are funny, don't you think, Grandfather?" The old man did not answer Kia, but only stroked his wispy beard thoughtfully. When Kia opened the little metal money box, Grandfather gasped in astonishment.

"So much money!" he exclaimed. Together, Kia and Grandfather counted the money and placed it in an empty coffee can kept at the back of Kia's closet. Carefully, Grandfather marked on a piece of paper how much money was in the can. "Thirty-five dollars and forty cents. It is a good beginning," he said, snapping the plastic lid on the can. He sat there for a long time cradling the can in his lap.

At last, Grandfather stood up and tucked his hands into the wide sleeves of his shirt. "Why does this woman care if we sell our vegetables or not? Does she think we can't sell them ourselves?"

"She was just being kind, grandfather," replied Kia.

Grandfather rocked back on his heels. "It seems an unusual thing for a stranger to do."

"But Hank is not a stranger, Grandfather. She and Sam are my friends." Kia remembered the day Hank told Kia how she worried about Sam spending day after lonely day in his apartment. "I think Hank did this for us because she knows that being different means you have to be braver than other people. Being brave sometimes

feels like an elephant is sitting on your heart."
She smiled up at Grandfather. "But friends can
make the elephant feel as light as a bird, don't
you think, Grandfather?"

Stroking her hand gently, the old man
said, "Kindness is like a well-fed crocodile that
lies quietly in the shallow river. Unless it emerges
from the water we do not think much about it.
But once it surfaces, we are on guard in case it is
hungry and wants to eat us. We do not think that
perhaps the crocodile is tired of the water and
just wants to bask in the sun. So it is with kindness. The ability to be kind lies within us all,
though like the crocodile buried in the mud, it is
not always in plain view. Then, when people are
kind to us we are afraid and suspicious of them,
when their desire is only to make us happy." His
voice sounded sad and far away. "It is only the
foolish and the ignorant who reject kindness."

Grandfather smiled, and clasping her
hand tightly in both of his, he said, "Neither
should I be like a crocodile buried in the mud. It
is time I met your good American friends to
thank them for what they did for us today."

Down the three long flights of stairs, Kia held tightly to Grandfather's hand. She recalled how they had walked the mountaintops hand in hand in search of herbs and plants.

"Are there mountains in this country, Grandfather?" she asked.

"Yes, but they are not near here and they are not like our mountains."

"Still, they are mountains," Kia replied confidently, "and all mountains are beautiful, no matter where they are. Maybe we can see them together some day." The old man did not speak, but squeezed Kia's hand a little tighter.

Hank answered the door in her waitress uniform. She smiled with pleasure when she saw Kia and Grandfather.

"You must be Kia's grandfather," she beamed. "She told me you were sick. Are you feeling better?"

With a slight nod, Grandfather said, "Thank you for how you help Kia."

Black eyes sparkling in amazement, Kia whirled toward her grandfather. He was speaking English!

Hank's cheeks turned pink beneath her golden hair. "Oh, it was nothing. I was glad to do it. Anything to shake up these people who think they're better than the rest of us. Right, Tiki?" The monkey had crept between Hank's legs and leaped into Kia's arms.

"Mom! Don't let Tiki out!" Sam skidded to a stop at the door when he saw Kia's grandfather. Embarrassed, Sam started to back away, but Hank put an arm around his shoulders and pulled him close.

"And I'll bet you've heard all about my son, Sam, one of the natural wonders of the world. Sam, this is Kia's grandfather, Mr. Vang." Bowing ever so slightly and looking the boy straight in the eyes, the old man held out his hand. It seemed like an eternity until Sam, after looking hard at Kia, slowly placed his stubby-fingered hand in the old man's dry, callused one.

"I hear about him," said Grandfather, stroking Tiki's tiny head. "He knows many tricks. You good teacher."

Sam blushed. "Oh, not really. He's just a smart monkey."

As they climbed the stairs, Kia exclaimed, "Grandfather! Why didn't you tell me you could speak English?"

With a shrug, Kia's grandfather replied, "Must you know everything, Little Cricket? Surely an old man like me can have a few secrets. You are getting too smart for your own good."

Just outside the door of their apartment, they heard Xigi speaking in a low, angry tone. Grandfather looked at Kia, then gave a little cough just loud enough for Xigi to know they were home. As they opened the door, Xigi was hanging up the telephone. Xigi's face looked tight, his eyes shadowed and anxious. Grandfather stopped and briefly locked eyes with Xigi, but neither spoke. Xigi looked away first, and the old man shuffled into the kitchen to start supper.

Kia started to follow her grandfather, then turned and said brightly, "Xigi, you will never guess what happened today." She told him about Hank's remarkable appearance at the market, but somehow the magic of the day was lost. Xigi remained tense, his eyes flitting about the room, looking everywhere but at her. Only when she said, "Come and look at how much money we made today," did he show any interest.

"Thirty-five dollars and forty cents," Xigi said in amazement as he counted the five- and one-dollar bills. "I can't believe you made that much money in one day. If you keep that up you'll be rich. People pay a lot for vegetables here." His face had relaxed and he seemed genuinely happy for Kia.

Kia smiled and dropped the money back in the can. She pushed the can to the far corner of her closet, where a dust ring marked the spot where it stood. "Yes, but we still need a lot more." In the kitchen across the hall, Kia heard water splashing into a kettle and a cover being placed upon it.

"Grandfather misses having you around," she said in a low voice. "So do I." She wanted to ask him where he was all the time, but she was afraid he would tell her it was none of her business. This was the first time during these long months that she and Xigi had sat together in such comfortable silence, and she did not want to destroy it. Still, she was as puzzled and as hurt as

Grandfather by Xigi's continual absence. In her heart, she also knew she was a little jealous that Xigi had so much time to himself.

"You must have many friends to be gone from home so much."

Xigi shrugged. "It's not hard to make friends. You and Grandfather need to get out more. You won't meet people sitting around here."

Throughout dinner Xigi talked about working at the school. He spoke the old language so Grandfather could understand him. "Greg Davis has really helped me. He's introduced me to a lot of his friends. We'll all be going to the same school this fall."

Grandfather kept piling more rice and vegetables on Xigi's plate, as if that would keep him home longer. Finally, Xigi laughed, looked at the clock, and said, "No more! I have to get ready to go." As Kia washed the dishes and Xigi went to change his clothes as he did every night, Grandfather walked down to the grocery store to see if Cha Lee was sitting outside. This was the first time Grandfather had left the house without Kia. She knew that having Xigi home for supper had made him feel better than any medicine could have. That night, Grandfather was again well enough to stitch his *pa ndau*.

Before she climbed into bed, Kia went to the closet to prepare the money box for their next trip to the market. She had to be sure they had enough coins and small bills to make change.

If she hadn't been so tired, she would have noticed the can wasn't exactly where she had left it. Even when she snapped off the lid and looked at the few pennies and nickels left rattling inside, she couldn't make herself believe the money was gone. In the dim light she stared into the can, then crawled to the far corner of the closet and ran her hands across the entire floor. Nothing. Nothing but dust and grit. For a long time she sat cross-legged on the floor clutching the empty coffee can. Not until she heard the familiar, faint sound of Grandfather humming in the still night air did she get up and walk woodenly to the bed. Tightly clutching her pillow, Kia stared out the window at the lights of the city. Loud music and laughter from a passing car momentarily drowned out Grandfather's quiet humming. The philodendron on the windowsill fluttered slightly in the cool breeze that did not reach the bed where Kia sat.

The next morning, outside the grocery store, old one-eyed Cha Lee reported that Shong Lue had gone home to his wife ranting and raving about going back to the old country.

"Guess what she told him?" Cha Lee grinned gleefully, the stumps of his teeth jagged and uneven. "Told him to go! Said she had found good work and liked it here and she was not going anywhere." Cha Lee rubbed his hands together in delight.

"What did Shong Lue say?" asked Grand-father. "A wife should not speak to her husband like that."

Old Cha Lee said, "If it was any other hus-band, I would agree. But Shong Lue is as full of hot air as the wind that blows across the desert. If his wife does not go back with him, he will stay here and continue complaining. He is too lazy to do anything else."

If she had not been so preoccupied with

the disappearance of the money, Kia would have told Cha Lee and Grandfather exactly how lazy Shong Lue was. But she had slept very little, and talking seemed too much effort.

"I have some good news, though," continued Cha Lee. "Shong Lue says he is done with the market. He says he will no longer go and have people snub his beautiful vegetables." Cha Lee turned his head toward Kia and grinned. "He says you brought him bad luck."

Before Kia could say anything, Cha Lee began to chortle. "And," he finished, "he sold me his truck, though it is little more than a junk heap."

"So," he continued, shaking his head, "now we have a truck but no driver. This market stuff is not so easy as in the old country."

That afternoon Kia was glad that the cooler temperatures had delayed further ripening of the vegetables. Although he was feeling better, Grandfather still tired easily. It would be a day or two before they would again haul their goods to the market. While Grandfather rested, Kia sewed her *pa ndau*, but anger at Xigi rippled through her.

Every day, except for a few hours when he helped at the school, he does what he wants while Grandfather and I work, Kia thought bitterly as she separated the colored thread. He spends time with us only when we have something he wants, like money, she fumed. Kia didn't know if she was sadder because the money was gone or because Grandfather had been so pleased to have Xigi home with them. This morning she had not told Grandfather about the missing money because she wanted to talk to Xigi first.

That afternoon Xigi came home as usual to change clothes. He greeted them cheerfully and did not seem to notice Kia's dark silence. Shortly after Xigi left the apartment, Kia told Grandfather she was going for a walk. It was not difficult for her to follow Xigi without his knowing. It was a lovely summer's day, and there were many people biking, playing ball, and pushing drowsy babies in strollers. Half a block ahead of her, Kia could see Xigi glancing at his watch as though he was late for wherever he was going. He probably doesn't want to keep his friends waiting, Kia thought bitterly.

Too bad he doesn't care that much about us.

After about eight blocks, Xigi hurried into a small grocery store. A warped, black screen door banged shut each time someone went in or out. Next to the curb was a fire hydrant. She crouched in the gutter behind the hydrant and in between two parked cars, eyes glued to the entrance of the store. She stayed there until her back was tired from hunching over, but still Xigi did not come out. Finally, she worked up enough nerve to peek in the large storefront window.

The inside of the store was dim compared to the blinding summer sun outside and Kia had to wait a few minutes for her eyes to adjust. A few customers wandered up and down the aisles putting things in red plastic carryall baskets. A heavy woman with very short white hair sat on a stool at the checkout counter watching some kids who were trying to decide what to buy at the candy display. A boy was sweeping in the rear of the store by the meat counter. He wore a white paper hat on his head and swept quickly and efficiently.

Confused, Kia thought Xigi must not have gone in the store after all. But where could he have gone? On one side of the store were a barbershop and a dry cleaner; on the other was a florist's and a small secondhand bookstore. After a quick look in each, she could see Xigi wasn't in either of them. He seemed to have vanished into thin air.

Reluctantly, Kia decided to return home. She glanced once more into the grocery store. The boy who had been sweeping had put the broom down and was handing a can of soup from a high shelf to an old man with thick glasses and trembling, spotted hands.

As she studied the boy's profile she realized the boy was Xigi.

She watched as Xigi directed the old man toward the woman at the checkout counter. He picked the broom up again to continue sweeping, but a deep voice from the rear of the store called, "Xigi! We have a delivery!" Kia scooted back to the very corner of the window, waiting to see what would happen next.

After a few minutes, Xigi started toward the door carrying two overflowing bags of groceries. As she crouched behind the fire hydrant,

Kia tripped over a skinny, black dog someone had tied to the hydrant. Thinking it had found a playmate, the dog thumped its whiplike tail and started licking the back of her neck. She grimaced and tucked her neck into her shoulders.

Balancing three bags of groceries and whistling softly, Xigi put his shoulder to the screen door and turned into the alley. The dog started to whine and yip as Kia got up to follow Xigi, and she held her breath, hoping Xigi would not turn to wonder at the commotion.

Parked behind the store was a small white truck with KOWALSKI'S MEATS in large red letters painted on the side. Kia watched in amazement as Xigi loaded the bags into the passenger seat, hopped into the driver's side, and drove away, his brown arm hanging casually out the window as if he'd been driving all his life. Speechless, Kia watched the truck head down the street until it was lost in traffic.

All the way home Kia kept wondering why Xigi would take the money they had earned from the market when he was making money of his own. And why did he not tell Grandfather he was working? And when did he learn to drive? He wasn't old enough to get his license. None of it made any sense. All Kia knew was that Xigi had to have taken the money, and she was going to find out why.

That evening Kia was unusually quiet. Grandfather, afraid she might be getting sick, kept feeling her forehead and looking into her eyes. Kia did not like keeping secrets from Grandfather, and she was relieved when the old man finally put his sewing aside and said it was time they both went to bed.

In her room Kia sat by the window waiting for Xigi to come home. She knew if she lay down she would never be able to stay awake. She tried counting the red cars and then the white cars, but it was too dark to tell the dark cars apart, so she gave up. Just when she thought she couldn't keep her eyes open one more second, the hinge on the apartment door squeaked. She tiptoed out to the kitchen where she found Xigi, head in his hands, slumped at the table. His head jerked up when he heard her, and Kia gasped when she saw his right eye was badly bruised and nearly swollen shut.

"Xigi! What happened to you?"

"What are you doing up, anyway?" he asked tiredly, cupping a hand around his injured eye. Kia went to the sink, soaked the dish towel in cold water, and handed it to him. He winced as he placed the towel over his eye.

"Maybe I should wake Grandfather," suggested Kia.

Shaking his head quickly, Xigi replied, "No, I'll be all right. It's only a black eye. No big deal."

Kia sat down on the edge of her chair across from Xigi, who stared back at her for a long while before sighing heavily and saying, "You might as well know that I took the money in the coffee can. I was going to give it all and more back to you tonight, but things didn't work out like I hoped."

Kia had no idea what Xigi was talking about, and her head felt fuzzy with tiredness. "What didn't work out, Xigi? I don't know what you mean."

Xigi walked over to the sink and rinsed the cloth in cold water. "Remember how at the camp in Thailand I could always pick the rooster that was going to win the fight and how I always won a lot of cigarettes I could sell? Everyone said I had a lucky streak because I was hardly ever wrong." Kia remembered the men who fought their roosters at night in a small pen at the outskirts of the camp. Kia had gone with Xigi only once to watch because the screeches of the fighting roosters and the wild urgings of the onlookers had sickened her.

"You've been fighting roosters?" Her voice was loud and shrill, and she was beginning to feel this was all a bad dream.

"Shhh, you'll wake Grandfather! No, Kia, I haven't been fighting roosters! Just be quiet and listen a minute." Xigi slid deeper into his chair before he continued. "The kid I clean at the school with, Greg Davis, asked me if I wanted to make some easy money. I thought about how hard you and Grandfather were working, so I said sure. I know you don't think I want Mother and Grandmother to come as badly as you, but I do. I thought since I was always so lucky, I could make some quick money to help bring them over here sooner. So, Greg introduced me to a bunch of his friends who taught me how to play poker."

"What's poker?"

"It's a card game, and you bet that the cards you have are better than the cards anybody else has."

"You bet for cigarettes like back at the camp?"

Xigi took the cloth away from his face. His eye was now just a puffy, purple slit in his face. "No. I bet money, and lots of it. Money I didn't have. I thought for sure I'd win every game I played, but I didn't. I lost more money than I had. And the people I owe it to don't want to wait for it."

It was now becoming clear to Kia why Xigi had been gone from home so much at night. "You weren't as lucky at poker as you were with the roosters, were you?"

For a horrible moment Kia thought Xigi was going to cry. His bottom lip quivered before he clamped it tightly between his teeth. He took a very deep breath. "No, and I still owe money. That's why I got this." He gestured toward his eye. "Guess I wasn't born so lucky after all."

"How much more money do you owe?"

"Almost a hundred dollars. And they want it now."

She and grandfather had thought thirty-five dollars was such a lot of money! To earn a hundred dollars, they would have to put in several long days at the market. "What are you going to do, Xigi?"

Xigi shrugged. "I wish I knew. It'll take me a long time to make that kind of money at the store." He laid his head down on his arm on the table.

It seemed so long ago that Kia had followed Xigi to the grocery store, she had almost forgotten about it. "I followed you today, Xigi. I know where you go in the afternoons now. How long have you been working there?"

"A couple of weeks." Xigi slowly raised his head. "Mostly I needed some money to start making bets. I was breaking even at first; then I don't know what happened. I started losing every game."

"But why did you keep on playing? Why didn't you quit before you owed so much money, Xigi?"

"I was sure I was going to start winning soon," he said in a flat voice. "But it never happened. I just kept losing. I don't know what happened," he said again.

It seemed to Kia there was only one thing to do. She licked her dry lips and said, "You know, you're going to have to tell Grandfather about this, Xigi."

"Yeah, I know. That's going to hurt a lot worse than this eye." Xigi stood up. "I've got to go to bed." He walked unsteadily out into the hallway toward his bedroom.

Kia started to follow, then grabbed his arm. "Wait—Xigi? Where did you learn to drive that truck?"

"I had to be able to drive to get the job at the store to deliver the groceries, so Greg gave me a few lessons in his father's car. It's not hard."

"You drove Mr. Davis's car? Does Mr. Davis know Greg let you drive?"

Xigi snorted. "Are you kidding? He thinks Greg is perfect. He'd be furious if he knew about it."

Shaking her head, Kia said, "Greg sure didn't seem like he could get you into all this trouble."

"I guess I got myself into it. Now I just don't know how to get out of it."

15

When Kia opened her eyes the next morning, she heard low voices in the living room. She could tell by the sun beating against the shade that it was much later than she usually woke up. Then she remembered all that had happened the day before. She slipped out of bed, walked quietly into the living room, and leaned against the far wall.

Grandfather was standing in front of Xigi, his thin face flushed and creased in anger.

"This is why you are always gone from home, to play this card game with your friends?"

Xigi flashed a look of impatience at his grandfather. "I told you. I thought I could make as much money in one night playing poker as you and Kia make in a week selling vegetables." Sagging back against the cushions of the sofa, Xigi added, "It just didn't work out the way I hoped."

"You sound like a foolish boy who thinks money can be obtained by wishing!" The old man rubbed his forehead. "Back home in Laos a man would be run out of the village for taking money that does not belong to him."

Kia remembered the day Xigi took little Wa to the fish pool and how Xigi had teased her about taking her to the edge of the village where the tigers roamed. She had not thought that would happen here in America, because tigers needed trees and tall grasses, not hard black streets and buildings that shut out the sun.

As though he had read her thoughts, Grandfather continued, "Cha Lee tells me they have jails in America with iron bars and cold cement walls. Is that where you want to go? If today you take money from your own family, Xigi, what will you do tomorrow?" Although his voice was low, the old man's sadness filled the room.

Xigi sat still as a stone. At last, Grand-father lowered himself into a chair. "Your father would not have let this happen to you," he said softly. "He would not have let you do as you please. It is my fault for what has happened. I did not know what to do, so I did nothing."

Kia ran to her grandfather and knelt down in front of him. She took his hands in hers. "It is not your fault, Grandfather. You are not to blame." A cloud passed in front of the sun, dark-ening the room.

At last, Xigi spoke. "She's right, Grand-father. What I did was not your fault. I just wanted to prove to you that I could do something on my own. I knew you wouldn't like me playing cards for money or working at Kowalski's when I could be helping you and Kia, but I don't want to sell vegetables the rest of my life!" Xigi's black eyes searched Grandfather's face. "You told Grandmother we were going to America so we could learn and grow. From now on I will try not to disappoint you."

Grandfather's eyes met Xigi's across the

room. Giving a slight nod and folding his hands together, he said, "Perhaps it is time the duckling leaves its nest to explore the world around him."

After a moment Xigi continued, "One thing I've learned is that money is not made easily, even in America. And now I'll probably lose my job at the store when Mr. Kowalski finds out I don't have a driver's license." Xigi's voice wavered.

"The job at the store means a great deal to you?" asked Grandfather softly.

Xigi began nervously cracking his knuckles. "Mr. Kowalski has been great. When business is slow and I've finished stocking the shelves and cleaning up, he teaches me how to cut meat. He said I'm a fast learner and in a few years I can work the meat counter with him."

Again the old man searched his grandson's face. "That is something you would like to do?"

"I think so. What I'd really like is to have my own store. Mr. Kowalski said there's no reason I shouldn't be able to as long as I learn all I can and don't cheat the customer." Kia could hear the mounting excitement in Xigi's voice sink in despair. "But I don't know if he's going to want me back after all this."

"Do you trust this Mr. Kowalski?" asked Grandfather.

Xigi shrugged. "He has been good to me."

Grandfather rose from his chair. "Then we will listen to what he has to say and do as he suggests."

"We? You mean you'll go with me?" Kia held her breath as she waited for Grandfather's answer.

"I will go with you if you will help me understand all that they say. This English is a difficult language to learn."

Kia watched from the window as Grandfather and Xigi walked down the street together for the first time in many months. Xigi is as tall as Grandfather, she noticed, as Xigi's dark, shaggy head leaned closer to Grandfather's white one to hear something he said.

Turning from the window, Kia looked closely at the philodendron plant Sam had given her. She couldn't see the line anymore where the old dirt had blended with the new. Tiny light green leaves were sprouting out all over. Sam was right. It was a tough little plant.

Even though the morning was half gone, Kia jumped back into bed and pulled the covers up over her head. Then she let out a joyful whoop before settling down and listening contentedly to the familiar hum of the car tires on the hot street.

That afternoon Kia and Sam watched Tiki, dressed in his little lemon-yellow vest and short pants, juggle marbles in Sam's apartment. His tiny round black hat, the size of a thimble, kept slipping over his eyes, but the monkey never faltered. Hank had gone in to work early with a bag full of Kia's vegetables.

"That Mr. Kowalski must be a really good guy to keep Xigi working for him and offer to loan him the money to pay those guys off right away," commented Sam drowsily. The cool morning had dissolved into another hot, muggy day, and Kia watched as the small fan ruffled Tiki's silky gray fuzz.

Kia felt slightly dizzy as her eyes followed the whirling marbles. "He say he take money from Xigi's check until all paid. Very mad that Xigi lie. Say Xigi bring trouble. Tell Xigi to keep nose clean." Kia looked questioningly at Sam. "Why nose be clean?"

Sam laughed. "It doesn't mean what you think. It just means Xigi had better not do anything else wrong."

Kia knew Xigi had been embarrassed by what he had done. "Guess anything that seems too good to be true is," he'd told Kia. "I don't think there is such a thing as good luck. You have to work for what you want." Yesterday Kia had seen the old yellow tablet lying open on top of Xigi's dresser. She hadn't seen it since they had arrived in America, and she hoped the pictures in his heart would come easily once more.

Suddenly Tiki flung the marbles aside and scampered to the top of Kia's head. He clung to her hair with his little fingers and hopped up and down. With an ear-piercing screech, he bent his fluffy gray head upside down over Kia's forehead and bared his pointed yellow teeth at her. Kia scrunched up her face and bared her teeth back at Tiki, who only screeched louder.

"You still going to take the bus to the market?"

Tiki's sharp claws scratched her scalp and Kia yelped. "Ow! Yes, it not bad. Grandfather better now."

Lifting Tiki gently off Kia's head, Sam said, "I still don't see why Xigi just didn't tell your grandfather he was working at the store. What's the big deal?"

"Because Xigi think Grandfather say he work at home before he work other place. Grandfather say family always first."

"Do you think that too?"

"I think," she began slowly, "Xigi way not bad way. But, Grandfather way not bad either." She folded her fingers together. "They need to mix ways to be right way."

Sam was quiet for a minute, then said, "Easier said than done. Trying to change is scary. Just ask me. I can tell you all about it."

She looked at her friend in genuine surprise. "You are afraid?"

"Oh, yeah, all the time."

"What of?"

Picking at a cuticle, Sam replied in a low voice, "Oh, I don't know. People, mostly, I guess. What they say, how they think about me."

Kia thought back to the day Hank had said that Sam was the only one who could decide if he was going to live his whole life in this apartment.

When she didn't say anything, Sam continued without looking up. His cuticle was ragged and nearly bleeding. "I know people don't mean to stare. I'd probably stare if I saw somebody like me, too. Hank used to say people would ignore me if I ignored them. But they didn't. They still pointed and turned around and felt sorry for me." He shrugged. "So, I just stay inside. It's easier. For both Hank and me."

Kia took a deep breath. She thought of the girls in the next building who whispered and laughed at her. And worst of all, she knew she would soon have to go to school and that there would be more kids who would make fun of her because she was different. In a small, shaky voice she said, "I afraid too. I wish I not go to school."

Now it was Sam's turn to be surprised.

"Whatever for? Once you get there you'll love it. I did, when I went."

"You don't go to school anymore?"

"Hank's been teaching me at home for five years, since I was eight. I only went to school until the third grade . . . until I started looking too different from the other kids. Then it wasn't fun anymore."

Kia looked at Sam's stubby arms and legs, his short, thick body. She never thought about Sam looking different. He was just Sam, her friend. She could not imagine him looking any other way.

Kia thought about Hank and how she worried about Sam. "Maybe your mother scared too?"

Sam tilted his head in surprise. "Why should she be?"

Lifting a shoulder, Kia replied, "Maybe we all scared. Maybe we scared for other people. Scared of things we not understand. Like Grandfather. He not understand ways different here than Laos. Maybe he not want to understand."

Sam heaved a deep sigh. "I guess things are always going to change no matter what. Nothing stays the same forever, does it?"

"No," said Kia quietly. "But sometimes it hard not to be afraid."

That evening before going to bed, Kia took out the creased magazine picture of the girl reading with her father. In Laos, when she had looked at the picture, she had been sure that when she got to America, the ring would make her feel as loved and happy as this girl. But as she slipped the ring on her finger, she felt shame and embarrassment.

She crumpled up the picture and threw it on the floor. Then she wrapped the small cloth around the ring and put it in an envelope. In her last letter, her mother had mentioned that Ia and her family were still waiting for sponsors so they could come to America. Kia knew Ia would never forgive her for taking the ring, but she knew she would never forgive herself if she didn't return the ring. On the outside of the envelope, she carefully wrote Ia's name and the address of the Ban Vinai camp that she had watched Thek write for them on letters to her mother and grandmother. She was sure Ia would know who had sent the ring.

16

The bus ride to the market the next morning was pleasant. Grandfather was happy today because yesterday Thek had brought a long letter that had arrived from Kia's mother. She said Grandmother was her old self and had even started going to the English classes at the camp. Kia smiled to herself when she heard that, because she knew Grandfather would now start going to the classes at the school so that Grandmother would not speak better English than he when she arrived. Each week now Grandfather went to the meetings at the church. He still did not like the English words and preferred to speak the old language when he was home, but after attending several meetings he told Kia, "It is a strange place, this America, where everybody's people come from someplace else. But," he added, smiling, "I think maybe that is what makes it such a good place."

As the bus stopped to pick up more riders, Kia said, "Isn't it sad, Grandfather, that Sam never goes outside because he's afraid people will stare and laugh at him? Hank said people called him a freak and told him he should be in a circus. Why do people do things like that, Grandfather?"

Grandfather winced as though someone had struck him. "If only mouths of people could be plugged like the mouths of jars. Remember, what people say, Little Cricket, is not important. It is how you act when they say these things that is important." Kia remembered Grandfather telling her that very same thing when Kao had called her a baby.

"But it still makes you hurt inside," she said. "Hank is afraid Sam will never go outside."

Nodding, Grandfather replied, "People say many things. It is up to each of us to decide what we do when people say such things. Sometimes we are the only ones who can help ourselves."

As they set up their table with the clean white cloth, Grandfather said, "I have had much time to think since coming to America. I remember a story my father told me when I was your age.

"There was once a blind man who was walking alone across an old bridge. Long ago, the blind man recalled, a deep creek had run beneath the bridge. The blind man had not crossed the bridge in years and since that time, the creek had dried up. People didn't walk across the bridge anymore, they just walked across the dry creek bed. But the blind man did not know this.

"When the man was in the middle of the creaky old bridge, his foot slipped through a board that had rotted. Terrified, he grabbed the fence railing with his right hand. Hanging with one hand, feet dangling, the blind man was afraid of tumbling into the rushing water below.

"'Help me!' he cried loudly. 'I'm blind and I am going to drown!'

"A man walking nearby heard him. He rushed up to the bridge to reassure the blind man.

"'Sir, don't be afraid. There is no water underneath you. If you just let go, it is less than a three-foot drop to completely dry ground.'

"The blind man did not believe or trust the passerby. 'I know why you want me to let go; so you can watch me fall into the water and have a good laugh at my expense. Thanks, but I am not that stupid.'

"He clung stubbornly to the railing and continued crying for help. The passerby shrugged his shoulders and went away.

"The blind man screamed for help until he was hoarse. Exhausted, he could no longer hold on. He squeezed his nose closed with his free hand, took a deep breath, and jumped.

"A moment later he found himself standing on dry solid ground. At first, he was immensely relieved. He was safe. But then his twisted ankle started to throb and he could barely stand.

"How foolish I was not to believe the passerby, he thought. If only I had trusted him I would not have hung there for such a long time preparing to drown. Now I can't walk and have no idea how I will get home."

Grandfather placed his *pa ndaus* on the table and smoothed them with his hand. "There are kind people no matter where one lives," he said. "We must learn to trust each other to make our lives good." Then, bending to set out the bags of vegetables, he began to hum quietly.

Under the market's yellow-striped canvas, the late August air was hot and still, and Kia could feel a trickle of sweat slip down her backbone. The knot of fear in her stomach started to melt like chocolate in the sun. Two vendors said hello when they were setting up, including the blond girl with the sea-green eyes. Many new customers as well as old customers had come to look at her stand today. They did not say more than hello, but Kia noticed they did not whisper among themselves as they had before. Now, some of them walked away carrying little brown lunch bags brimming with vegetables that Kia and Grandfather had carefully packed.

In the park across the street from the market, children splashed in the fountain where the bronze sculpture of an Indian maiden stared into the hazy distance beyond the Mississippi River. A flock of pigeons with shining green-and-purple necks swooped to the ground near them.

Kia found an empty bench and stretched out on it. Overhead, great puffs of clouds floated lazily across the blue sky. When she was little, her mother had often stopped her work in the fields to point to passing clouds and exclaim, "See! A cow with the trunk of an elephant!" Or, "Look, Kia, how the rooster runs to get away from that tiger!" Today Kia did not see any elephants or roosters. But she knew when her mother came, they would together look at the clouds and see new things, things they had never before dreamed.

Summer was almost over, and the can in the closet had been filled and deposited in a bank account many times over. Mr. Davis had showed them how to do this, and their savings account was growing steadily. Every week, after Mr. Kowalski paid Xigi and took out some of the money Xigi owed him, Xigi would put half of his money into the can, too. At first, he wanted to put all the money he earned into the can, but Grandfather insisted Xigi keep some out for himself.

"You are working hard and there will be things you will want to buy," Grandfather had told him. "When school starts, you will not be able to work so many hours, so you should save some of your money."

Kia also was given money to spend, but she saved most of hers. She didn't think she would ever again buy anything without thinking of the ring she had taken from Ia.

Mr. Davis had stopped by the night before and said arrangements had been made for her mother and grandmother to join them by the end of September. When Grandfather had proudly presented the money they had saved all summer, Mr. Davis was amazed.

"How did you manage to save this much?"

Xigi and Kia had looked at Grandfather, who said, "It is what we work for."

Shaking his head, Mr. Davis had given the money back to Grandfather. "The church has raised enough money to bring them here. Why don't you keep this and buy some things you need?"

Grandfather had looked at the money and handed it back at Mr. Davis. "When they come, we have everything we need."

Kia wondered, if their father had been with them, would Xigi still have gotten into trouble? Would their father have been firmer with Xigi than Grandfather had been, so he would have had less free time? But, she realized, remembering the ring she had taken, if someone is determined to do something, no one else can really do anything to stop it.

Gazing across the river, Kia noticed one tree that wore a crown of vibrant orange. That, she thought to herself, is how she would stand out from the other kids at school. The flaming tree reminded her of Hank, strong and colorful, who was not like anyone she had ever known. She smiled to herself as she imagined what her quiet mother would think of Hank.

Sam had told her that the trees would change colors, to glowing reds and yellows, before the snow fell. When she had told her grandfather this, he had shaken his head and declared there must be magic in this country, too.

Shortly before the market closed, a tall woman with long, slim fingers stopped at their table. She picked up and carefully examined one of grandfather's *pa ndaus*. Her lashes made delicate spiked shadows beneath her eyes.

"What lovely embroidery!" she exclaimed. Looking at Grandfather, she asked, "Did you do this?"

Grandfather nodded and took a step closer to her. A little girl eating a peach walked up to the woman. Peach juice dribbled down the child's chin onto her shirt and down her sticky arms. She started licking the juice from her wrists until her mother handed her some tissues. Kia, sharply reminded of her cousin Wa, smiled at the little girl.

The woman paid Grandfather for the *pa ndau*. Kia watched her walk away and was surprised to see the two girls who lived in the next apartment building waiting for her. The girls stood next to each other, glancing quickly from the *pa ndau* the woman showed them back to Kia and Grandfather's table. Then Kia did something she had longed to do all summer. She waved at them. The girls just stared at her. Smiling broadly this time, Kia waved again. Confused, the girls glanced at one another. At last, one girl, then the other, raised a limp hand toward Kia before turning to walk with the woman.

As they packed up to go home that afternoon, Grandfather said, "Little Cricket, I have never seen a monkey in a yellow vest and black hat juggle. Perhaps your friend Sam would come and show me what this amazing creature can do."

"Oh, wait until you see him, Grandfather!" exclaimed Kia. "He makes so much noise for something so tiny. . . ." She stopped abruptly and looked questioningly at her grandfather. "You mean, ask him to come to our house?"

The old man nodded.

Kia began folding the white cloth. Without looking up, she said, "I do not think he will come."

"Perhaps not. But that is a decision you must let him make."

Kia placed the cloth on the top of her basket. "This afternoon I will go and tell Sam you would like to see his monkey juggle."

Grandfather walked to Kia and cupped her small face in his brown hands. "For such a Little Cricket, you are a very good friend."

AUTHOR'S NOTE

The Hmong are some of the most recent arrivals of immigrants to the United States. The word *hmong* means "free." Although the story of Kia Vang and her family is fictional, it is based on fact.

Originally from China, the Hmong can be traced as far back as 2700 B.C., when they are mentioned in Chinese historical records as a "people on the move." They settled in Indochina about 1810, eventually moving into Vietnam, Laos, and finally, Thailand. The Hmong survived for thousands of years by farming, living without electricity or indoor plumbing.

During the Vietnam War, many of the Hmong were recruited by the U.S. Army as a special guerilla force to fight the Communists. When the United States pulled out of Vietnam, the Hmong became direct targets of persecution by the newly established Lao People's Democratic Republic and were once more forced to move. They began arriving in the United States in 1976. Today, California, Minnesota, and Wisconsin have the highest population of Hmong.

The Hmong had no written language until 1950. Their exceptionally rich culture was kept alive through storytelling and the oral tradition.

Living in America has been especially difficult for the older generation of Hmong. When they first arrived in the United States, they were not settled together, and this caused severe depression and cultural shock until they were resettled to live among relatives and friends.

Today, at the farmers' market in St. Paul, Hmong families just like Kia's can be found selling their vegetables and beautiful handicrafts.

Each summer, over the Fourth of July, between 20,000 and 30,000 people from around the country gather in St. Paul for the annual Minnesota Hmong Sports Tournament.

Since their arrival in America, opportunities in education have expanded and enriched their lives. Among those who have made great contributions to our country is Senator Mee Moua of Minnesota, who was the first Hmong legislator in the United States.

As with other immigrants who have and will continue to make their homes in America, the Hmong help make our country a fascinating and exciting place to live.

HOW TO PRONOUNCE HMONG WORDS

The pronunciation of Hmong is very complex—
there are thirteen vowels and fifty-six consonant
sounds in the Hmong language. Like Chinese,
and like many other languages in Southeast Asia,
such as Thai, Vietnamese, and Lao, Hmong is
also a *tonal* language, which means that every syllable has a specific pitch level or melodic shape.
The same combination of sounds can mean different things depending upon the tone with
which it is pronounced. It is the tonal system that
gives languages like Hmong their musical,
singsong quality.

Below are just a few hints to help you with the Hmong words and names in this book. To learn more about the Hmong language, and to hear Hmong speakers saying words and phrases in their language, you can go to this Web site:

ww2.saturn.stpaul.k12.mn.us/hmong/
pronunciation.html

- When a Hmong word ends in *b, j, g, s, v, m,* or *d,* these final letters are never pronounced. Instead, they indicate the seven different tones in the Hmong language. The name for one of the shamanic rituals that Kia's grandfather performs, the *hu plig,* sounds something like "hoo plee." *Tauj,* the word for a kind of grass Kia's mother uses to make brooms, is pronounced "tau" (rhymes with *cow*).

- The letter *x* sounds like *sh* in English. Kia's brother's name, Xigi, sounds like "Shee-gee," with a hard *g*. The name *Xiong* sounds like "Shiong."

- The letter *q* is like a *k* sound, but far back in the throat. The name for the Hmong bamboo mouth organ that Kia's grandfather plays, the *qeej*, sounds like "kay."

- *Th* does not sound the way it does in English, but like a *t* uttered with a small puff of air. The name *Thek* sounds like "Tek."

- The combination *ue* is pronounced as one syllable. The Lue in the names *Uncle Lue* and *Shong Lue* sounds like "Lweh."

- In combinations of consonants beginning with *n*, the *n* sound is not a separate syllable. The word for the famous Hmong story cloths, like the ones Grandfather embroiders, *pa ndau*, sounds like "pah ndow."

SUGGESTED FURTHER READING

To learn more about the Hmong people and their stories, look for the books listed below, or visit the St. Paul Hmong Cultural Center Web site: www.hmongcenter.org.

A Hmong Family. By Nora Murphy. With photographs by Peter Ford. (Lerner Publications Company, Journey Between Two Worlds Series, 1997.)

Dia's Story Cloth: The Hmong People's Journey of Freedom. By Dia Cha. Illustrated by Chue Thao Cha and Nhia Thao Cha. (Lee & Low Books, 1998.)

Farmer Boy. By Peggy Mathews. (Pacific Asia Press, 1996.)

Farmer's Market: Families Working Together. By Marcie R. Rendon. With photographs by Cheryl Walsh Bellville. (Carolrhoda Books, 2001.)

Fighters, Refugees, Immigrants: A Story of the Hmong. By Mace Goldfarb. (Carolrhoda Books, 1982.)

How the Farmer Tricked the Evil Demon. By Alice Lucas, translated by Ia Xiong. In English and Hmong. Illustrated by Kosal Kong. (Pacific Asia Press, 1994.)

Jouanah: A Hmong Cinderella. By Jewell Reinhart Coburn and Tzexa Cherta Lee. Illustrated by Anne Sibley. (Shen's Books, 1996.)

Nine-In-One Grr! Grr!: A Folktale from the Hmong People of Laos. As told by Blia Xiong, adapted by Cathy Spagnoli. Illustrated by Nancy Hom. (Children's Book Press, 1993.)

The Making of Monkey King. By Robert Kraus and Debby Chen. In English and Chinese. Illustrated by Wenhai Ma. (China Books and Periodicals.)

The Whispering Cloth: A Refugee's Story. By Pegi Deitz Shea. Illustrated by Anita Riggio and You Yang. (Boyds Mills Press, 1996.)